THE BRIGHTEST LIGHT

ALASKAN HEARTS, BOOK 2

MELISSA STORM

Editor: Megan Harris
Proofreaders: Jasmine Bryner & Becky Muth

Partridge & Pear Press
PO Box 72
Brighton, MI 48116

ABOUT THIS BOOK

Anchorage librarian Scarlett Cole has always preferred to live out her adventures within the pages of her favorite books. That all changes when she befriends junior musher Lauren, who presents her with the opportunity of a lifetime —stop reading about the Iditarod and actually get out there to race!

With her career now on the line and only one chance to establish herself amongst the dog-sledding community, Scarlett knows she'll need to work hard and with no regrets. Unfortunately, another new racer quickly sets his sights on her, vowing to triumph at any cost... even if his techniques aren't quite above board.

When Scarlett and her new rival receive a flurry of media attention, they discover that succeeding in the race could mean losing big in life. Just how much is Scarlett willing to risk to make her lifelong dream come true?

AUTHOR'S NOTE

Do you believe in fate?

I sure do.

Let me tell you about two very important things in my life that just seem to perfectly planned to have happened as a fluke.

The first is one I talk about often—my love story with Mr. Storm. He's definitely my soul mate, but he's not my first husband. I never pictured myself as a divorcee, especially in my 20s. But some of us need a little more time to grow up and find ourselves. Try telling any young adult that they aren't quite there yet!

I started dating my first husband at 19, we married when I was 23, and divorced at 27. I learned a lot from that time in my life, as painful as it was. Because as I continued to grow, mature, and find myself, my then husband's love for me seemed to fade with each passing day. In what felt like the blink of an eye, we went from adoration to derision. Our marriage became a very uncomfortable place to be, full of cruel words and angry directives fired at me when I least expected them.

And all because I had found what I was meant to do in this world: write my books and start businesses to help other writers live their dreams, too.

I was so angry at how things turned out. What was love? Surely, it was a made-up Hollywood phenomena since my own romance had crashed and burned so brutally.

But then on the heels of that dark time, I met a man—a writer like me—who had just moved to my state all the way from Alaska. He left everything behind to pursue his dreams of being an author. I'd left so much behind because achieving my dreams meant I'd lost the love of a man who had vowed to love me until death do us part.

I definitely wasn't going to go to that place again.

And yes, Mr. Storm worked his way right into my heart. First as an online acquaintance, then a friend, and at last a husband. We met in early August, realized the love brewing between us in September, and eloped on December 1 of that same year.

Five years later, we are living our dreams together along with our gorgeous daughter who is the realization of the greatest dream of all.

The thing is, if he hadn't been brave enough to leave his life and decide to move thousands of miles away on a whim, and if I hadn't taken that incredibly scary leap to leave my marriage and then to let love in again, we wouldn't be where we are today.

There are so many other little pieces about our story that prove God had His eyes on us—far too many to enumerate here, which is why one day I plan to write our full love story in a pair of novels, *The Legend of My Love* and *My Love Will Find You*.

Until then, I continue to weave pieces of our story into each and every book I write. Love changed everything for me, and finding it at last is what encouraged me to write in the Romance genre. Because how could I not believe in love when I live it every day? How could I not want to share that joy with others? To offer hope and proof that—*yes*—it's out there?

So that's my first big tale of destiny. The other is one I haven't told anyone until now, but I'd like to tell you.

Growing up, I always felt like an outsider. Maybe because I preferred books and animals to people, which made me different and awkward in school. Maybe because I didn't really know my bio dad and was only a "half" among my siblings. It could have been so many things.

But that uncomfortable, uncertain feeling followed me

my whole life. It became even more apparent in college, when I changed my major not just once, but eleven times!

Feeling lost and confused, I prayed to God. *What should I do my life? What am I here for?*

And, reader, I heard His voice so clear in that moment along with a flash of flame before my eyes that only lasted a second but sure got my attention.

"Write."

There was no arguing with that directive. I'd always loved books—reading them, attempting and failing to write my own. But now God had told me clearer than I'd ever understood anything in my life until then, that I was meant to live this crazy, impossible dream.

Like I said, there was no arguing with that.

So instead, silly young me, I ignored it.

I chose a major, graduated with highest honors, went straight through graduate school on a special research fellowship, accepted a good job when I was done.

I would proudly tell anyone who would listen, "Yes, I wanted to be a writer, but I'm far too pragmatic for that. I need a job that will pay the bills, thank you very much."

Less than a year after that crazy rush, God reminded me of what I was supposed to do with my life. A newspaper in the area reached out to me online because of my participation in a book club and asked if I'd consider writing reviews and covering local events for them.

The dream was still alive in my heart, even if I had silenced it in my mind, so I eagerly agreed. Less than a month after that, they promoted me to lead Books Contributor and gave me a weekly column—and money!

It wasn't much, but I was officially being paid for a talent I had undervalued my whole life. This was the confidence boost I needed to start my first novel.

And, honestly, it felt like coming home.

It only took me three months to write that first book, which is now, after much revision, published as *A Colorful Life*.

Now that I'd managed the impossible—writing an entire book—I was hooked. I also discovered a talent for online marketing and started my first business to help other authors find their readers.

It took off like a shot, enabling me to quit the day job very early in my author career. I've been living this life for over eight years now, and I wouldn't change a day of it.

That's the thing about fulfilling your destiny...

Even when it's hard, it's still meant to be.

I am so grateful for my dual acts of fate—and faith from a God who believed in me even when I forgot how much I believed in Him.

CHAPTER 1

SCARLETT WATCHED UNTIL LAUREN'S SLED BECAME NOTHING more than a pinpoint on the horizon. Her best friend had found a new life living amongst the world Scarlett longed to join for herself.

Ever since she had accepted the job as an Anchorage librarian and moved from her tiny hometown in Texas all the way north, the Iditarod had been one of Scarlett's foremost passions—along with books, of course. And now she was here, best friends with one of the top racers to watch... but watching from the sidelines.

To her, the snow glimmered with magic, the winds hinted at adventure, and helping the dogs fulfill their purpose gave her one of her own. The main problem, of course, was that dog sledding was not a sport that could be taken up casually. Her friend, Lauren, had left everything about her old life behind when she chose to become a handler for the infamous Shane Ramsey, who had since transformed into her doting husband and committed race coach.

But none of that exactly helped to bring Scarlett clarity.

Could she really starve one passion to feed another? Ultimately, racing for herself would mean quitting her job as a librarian, possibly to never return. Books were just too special for her to willingly cast aside.

She still fondly remembered herself as a five-year-old girl hanging on the arm of her papa's recliner as he taught her how to sound out the words splashed across the front page of the local *Sentinel.* She'd learned so much more than how to read—she'd learned the power of stories, the power of words.

Writing these words herself had never been on the table. She preferred to live out her adventures, either vicariously or in reality, which was what had also drawn her to the great race as she'd begun to learn about her new home state.

Now that she was also best friends with an actual musher, Scarlett's longing intensified. She'd always been happy to live between the pages, but now she craved the open air, the rushing winds, the slick drive across the snow.

Lauren was so happy, and Scarlett knew *she* could be, too. But she also didn't know how to bring this dream into actuality. Perhaps she would figure it out one day, or perhaps she would forever be stuck between two worlds, not knowing to which she truly belonged.

Her phone buzzed in her coat pocket, and she bit the thumb of her glove to pry it off her hand so she could press the teeny, tiny button to answer.

"Scarlett, you're going to have to go without me," her friend, Liz, announced without preamble.

"Without you? But we go together every year!" she argued, referring to the Miners and Trappers Ball that celebrated the start of the annual race.

"I know, I know. I'm so sorry." At least Liz did sound genuinely apologetic about the last-minute change of plans. "I would be there if I could, but something has come up."

This wasn't like her usually reliable friend, and that worried her. "Is everything okay?" Scarlett asked, fearing the worst.

"Yeah, it will be fine. I'll tell you more when I know more. I wouldn't cancel if it weren't important. You know that."

"I do, and don't worry about me. I can hang out with Shane and Rosie."

"Oh, pfffhew. Good. Okay. I'll talk to you later. Have a great time at the ball, Cinderella!"

Scarlett laughed as they hung up. She and Liz Benjamin had made fast friends almost immediately after Scarlett arrived in town. Her father, Ben Benjamin, served as one of the race officials and always had the best access to insider events, like the Miners and Trappers Ball. Liz had never much cared for racing, having grown up with it as a constant, but she was happy to help indulge Scarlett's interests.

That's what good friends did, after all. And as a good friend, Scarlett needed to feel happy for Lauren rather than envy her success.

With one last glance toward the horizon where she had last seen Lauren and the other racers charge forth toward Nome, she buried the piece of her heart that belonged to this sport and headed home to find a good book to cozy up with for the night.

Tomorrow was the ball, and she wouldn't miss it for the world.

CHAPTER 2

SCARLETT PLACED A HAND ON HER STOMACH AND SUCKED IN a deep breath as she stood outside the hall, working up the nerve to go inside. She'd attended the ball for the past few years, but never on her own.

Shane had texted earlier to let her know he'd be late. His ex-wife was creating trouble when it came to collecting their daughter, Rosie, and he'd promised the little girl she could come and be a princess for the night.

This meant Scarlett was totally alone, except for the sea of acquaintances that flanked her on every side—not all of them recognizable in their costumes to match this year's theme.

Dressing up had never been required for the ball, but Scarlett had always thrown herself into the theme full-force. Last year they'd gone as glammed up lumberjacks, and the year before they arrived dressed in homage to Buzzwinkle, the local trouble-making moose.

Oh, the compliments they'd received that time!

For tonight, they had planned sexy Yeti costumes. Scarlett's was far more modest than Liz's, but she still felt awkward about arriving alone in such a bold getup. Instead, she'd opted for a floor-length formal gown she had worn as a bridesmaid a few years back.

She inhaled another deep breath as she reached into her tiny clutch purse and pulled out her hulking iPhone. Activating selfie mode, she checked her makeup and hair, both of which were definitely overdone upon second glance. As much as she enjoyed socializing, she was by nature an introvert and spending time with people she only knew in passing quickly exhausted her.

Breathe in.

She held the air inside her lungs as she broke through the throngs at the entry and into the main event. She let her breath out again once she'd confirmed that everyone's eyes hadn't drifted toward and then stayed with her. Silly to think that everyone would stop enjoying themselves to stare her way, but that kind of thing often happened in books, so it felt like a real enough possibility.

Just in case, she took a slow, sweeping view of the hall, only to notice that her fears were not entirely unfounded. In the far corner, she spotted an unfamiliar face fixed intently on her. Scarlett didn't recognize him despite her obsession with the sport and general familiarity with its players, and she doubted he recognized her.

No, if she'd met this man before, she would certainly remember. Everything about him had obviously been arranged to leave an impression. His dark hair was heavily styled into a sleek wave above his forehead. The tuxedo he wore was meticulously pressed and perfectly matched the shoes that shone proudly on his feet. The plaid kerchief tucked into his pocket was the only indication he'd considered the night's Northern theme.

Scarlett felt like a fish out of water as she glanced down at her dark purple gown with faux jewels laid boldly along the neckline. She'd worked her white blonde hair into a French twist and borrowed a pair of big dangly chandelier earrings to go with it.

And the stranger's eyes were *still* on her. She felt them as she walked toward the open bar and requested a lime and seltzer.

She felt them as she found her assigned table and took a seat. Even still, she felt them as she checked her text messages for an update from Shane.

When at last she could take it no more, she decided she'd rather have a few very awkward minutes of confrontation than an entire evening spoiled by his unforgiving gaze.

She rose suddenly before she could change her mind,

snagging the bottom of her gown on the chair's leg but thankfully not falling or tearing it in the process.

Making direct eye contact, she strode over to him, hoping she looked as confident as he seemed to feel. For the seemingly endless eternity of her walk along the edges of the dance floor, his eyes remained on her, tracking each step. His face gave away nothing.

Scarlett needed to know why.

CHAPTER 3

SCARLETT'S HEELS CLACKED AGAINST THE MARBLE FLOOR AS she pressed through the crowd in her attempts to reach the enigmatic stranger who'd thus far refused to let her out of his sight.

A wan smile inched from one of his cheeks to the other as at last she came to stand face-to-face with him.

Now that she was closer, she saw that his eyes were mismatched. She'd read about the rare and enviable trait of heterochromia, but had only ever seen in dogs and cats before tonight.

One crystalline blue eye resembled the sky on a sunny day. The other swirled with bright amber and green. She didn't know where to look or what to say.

And he seemed in no hurry to help her out. Placing a hand inside his suit jacket, he continued to watch her—to wait. His smile slowly broadened like a flower opening its petals to face the sun. Not just any flower, though—something carnivorous or with thorns. She honestly didn't know whether she felt intrigued or enraged by his easy confidence, especially since it was so opposite to her own nature.

She took in a deep breath and widened her stance to ground herself, make sure she didn't lose her nerve and run away before learning more. The sweet scent of lavender and honeysuckle flooded her nostrils. Was this him? It felt so at odds with what she saw standing before her that she lost hold of the tirade she'd prepared on her way over.

A heat rose to her cheeks, and she knew they must be burning as bright red as her name. What was she doing? Why was she still standing there speechless? Why had this strange man already gotten so far under her skin?

There was only one way to find out...

"Do I know you?" she demanded, her voice meeker than she'd hoped, but at least she'd said something now.

"Not yet," he answered glibly, removing his hand from his jacket and extending it toward her. "But you will."

Startled, she accepted by placing her own newly manicured hand into his. All the air whooshed from her lungs as he pulled her in tight to his chest.

Things like this didn't happen to Scarlett Cole. This right here was straight out of a book, straight out of many books. It wasn't how her real life was lived. She was a small-town librarian, not a wealthy debutante, and definitely *not* a member of the royal family.

Still, in that moment she became a living princess.

An angry princess.

"You didn't say please," she pointed out as he walked her toward the center of the dance floor and moved them seamlessly into a dance.

Oh, what a childish thing to say at such a grownup moment, she chided herself. Yet somehow it felt better than saying nothing at all. Words were her only power against this overpowering man, and she needed any that managed to come to her.

"I didn't know I needed to," he answered with a chuckle, the two clashing colors of his right eye seemed to dance along with them.

"Who are you?" She tensed in his arms upon realizing that she knew nothing about her new dance partner, only that he was here and his very presence did strange things to both her mind and body.

His answer came fast and smooth like the tracks on a sled across fresh snow. "A handsome stranger."

"Tell me your name," she rasped, feeling her words leaving her once again. As much as they comforted her, they gave her no strength. He paid them no heed.

He smiled across at her, for in her heels, she easily matched his height. Their eyes locked as he declared, "It's not important. Just dance."

And so they did.

And Scarlett fell more and more under his indomitable spell as the music carried them through the night.

CHAPTER 4

As the man with no name moved Scarlett across the dance floor, she felt her tension lighten and eventually float away into the tall ceilings above. Some moments were a gift for the future, ones meant to look back on often and relive fondly. Others, like this night, were gifts of the present. They needed to be enjoyed while they lasted and then pushed to the back archives of the mind, retrieved if and when it ever became necessary to look back.

She silenced her voice, a feat on its own, but even more remarkably, she let her thoughts rest as well. In that moment, she belonged to the music, to this stranger, to the night.

He pulled her closer, bringing his lips to her ear. "You want to kiss me," he informed her.

And she realized that maybe she did but wasn't sure how she felt about him announcing it to her like this, especially considering they'd only just met that evening.

She shifted subtly in his arms. Her body wanted to conform to his will, but everything in her spirit now resisted.

The spell was broken.

"How do you know what I want?" She pulled back to add distance between them. It was the only way to make sure her body didn't rebel and kiss him anyway as he'd so boldly suggested.

"It's written all over your face, in every curve of your body. I'm simply putting words to the feeling. It's one we share."

She shook him off when he tried to resume the dance. "I'm not sure why," she hissed, "but I thought you were a gentleman. I do what I want when I want, not when I'm told by some guy who won't even give me his name."

"Relax. You've misunderstood me." He tried to take her in his arms again, and she pulled away again.

As her rage grew, her power returned. The shy, wilting Scarlett had officially left the building, and in her place was the girl who was used to being the heroine of every story, especially her own.

"Stop. I no longer wish to dance," she said, jabbing a

finger into his broad chest. "That'll show me to dance with a man who can't even ask appropriately. Have a good rest of your night."

She stormed off through the crowd, the others too lost in their own enjoyment to notice the passing tempest.

He did not pursue her. Still, his eyes weighed heavily on her as she moved across the hall, trying to cut loose the anchor of desire that tied her to him.

"Scarlett!" a little voice cried as it raced toward her, and its speaker clasping small arms around her hips.

"Sorry we're so late," Shane Ramsey said. "Isabel..." As he mentioned his ex-wife's name, he gave Scarlett a look that luckily escaped Rosie's notice. His ex had a way of ruining all the most special moments between the father and daughter, and she doubted Shane was even still surprised by that maddening woman's interference. Scarlett certainly wasn't.

"Who was that you were dancing with when we came in?" Shane asked, looking over her shoulder and back down the path she had just blistered through the room.

She turned, feeling the chain that tied her to the mystery man break as if it were a physical sensation. When she looked back to the place where she'd left her suitor, he was no longer there.

Well, whoever he was, that would be the last she needed to worry about him. The night would soon come to a close, and she wanted to spend the rest of it making good memories with the people she loved.

And that did not—could not ever—include him.

CHAPTER 5

SCARLETT SLEPT IN THE NEXT MORNING, CHOOSING TO SKIP church and catch up on rest. Funny that she'd chosen to forgo services on the day she most felt she needed to repent. Her reaction to the charming stranger had been almost animalistic, and thinking of it now, she felt as if she'd done something wrong by agreeing to dance with him.

No, Scarlett wasn't one of those crazy folks from that town in *Footloose*. She absolutely loved to dance, to live her life to the fullest. Only last night she'd felt full in a different way—and it bothered her.

Perhaps she could call home and talk to her old friend Elise about all this. They had been thick as thieves until Scarlett had declared her intention to leave Texas and pursue greater adventure. Her high school friends never understood her desire for more, nor did they understand how she intended to get by working as a librarian in Alaska.

But her friend was a youth pastor now and would surely have more experience dealing with hormonal surges like the one that had coursed through Scarlett's body last night.

Could she bring herself to admit what she'd felt? Could she even put it into words?

Hmm... Hopefully she'd have more clarity after a cup of coffee or two. She pulled herself out of bed and made her way into the kitchen, her goldfish pajama pants picking up dust as she walked. How long had it been since she'd last given this place a good sweep?

Too long, obviously. She mentally added this new task to her lengthening list for the day.

In the kitchen, she found her favorite vanilla brew coffee and popped a K-Cup into the machine. Next, she fished a croissant from the bread drawer and lathered it with a generous slab of butter.

Already, she began to feel more human as she left yesterday behind and forged a new path for today.

It was just an adventure, just a one-time, weird thing, she told herself as she heated a bit of milk in the microwave. Back in her bedroom, her phone jingled with the ringtone she'd set for Liz.

Calling to get all the gossip now, are you? She smirked at how well she knew her friend and realized that her current conundrum wouldn't even exist if Liz had gone to the ball with her as planned.

"Hey," Scarlett croaked into the phone, using her voice for the first time that day and hating how it sounded.

"Scar, quick! Turn on the TV!" her friend shouted, and the sound shot straight to Scarlett's brain, forming an insta-headache.

"Do you have to be so loud before I've had my coffee?" she grumbled, tracing her way back to the living room and searching for the remote.

"Do you see it yet?"

"My remote? No."

Liz let out an impatient sigh. "This is important, Scar! Just push the button on the TV set."

"Fine." Scarlett walked up to the TV and felt around under the flat screen surface to find the power button. "What chann—?"

Her question was immediately cut off when the screen flickered to life, only to reveal her mysterious suitor from the night before.

"Liz! How...?" So many thoughts fought for her attention that all Scarlett could do in that moment was gasp as she watched the familiar face speak unheard words on the local news station.

"Keep watching. There's footage of you, too."

She frantically felt for the volume buttons. What was he

saying? How did Liz know him? And why would there be footage of Scarlett?

"I would've come if I'd known you needed me there to keep you out of trouble," her friend said gently, then exploded again. "I can't believe you spent all night flirting with Henry Mitchell, III!"

At last he had a name, and surprisingly, it was one she already knew. Dread pooled in her stomach, hot and bitter like the coffee that sat losing steam in her kitchen. She wanted to vomit.

"Mitchell? As in…?"

"Yes, yes, that's him! His grandfather is the first, his dad is the second—"

"And he's the third," Scarlett finished, immediately understanding why she'd felt such a severe case of ick upon waking up that day.

Now more than ever, she hoped she would never see this man—this Henry Mitchel, III—again.

But first she wanted to hear what he had to say and learn why her face was splashed all over the news.

CHAPTER 6

SOMEHOW SCARLETT'S HEART MANAGED TO FLUTTER AT THE same time her blood reached its boiling point. So many mixed emotions it was making her sick.

Liz's dapple Akita, Samson, broofed in the background, trying to get her attention. "Hush, boy! We'll take your walk in a minute!"

Both women watched as the news continued their feature of last night's ball and, most of all, its most mysterious guest.

"Did you know?" Liz whispered, so that neither of them would miss what was being said on the news. So far, they hadn't learned much of anything, just regurgitated facts that everyone already knew about the Mitchell family.

"That he was related to that horrible man? Of course not!" Scarlett protested, shuddering as she ran through all the awful things Henry's grandfather had done to the sport, the dogs, the environment, the city.

Everything he'd touched had turned to a sad, lifeless gray. The hundreds of dogs in his care had been recovered with large welts on their backs, visible ribs sticking out from their sides, and many other signs of both neglect and torture. Although he'd housed over three-hundred dogs, only one handler and a small yard had been dedicated to their care. In his eyes, having the dogs had been profitable, but looking after them properly had not been.

Henry Mitchell, Sr., had lived his entire life with an eye on profit and fame. And he had gained heaps of both, but at the expense of his soul.

Regarded as one of the cruelest men in recent memory, he'd been out of the public eye for the last few, refreshing months. And how could his grandson, his own flesh and blood, be any different? Something in Scarlett had known. Oh, if only she had Hermione's time-turner to erase that night they'd spent in each other's arms.

"I thought he was banned from the race and all related events," Liz murmured.

"Obviously, that ban did not extend to his family." Scarlett shuddered again as the footage looped and at last she caught sight of herself staring doe-eyed into that debonair devil's mismatched eyes.

"You looked really good last night, even if you didn't end up going as a sexy Yeti," Liz said unhelpfully.

"*Shh*, I want to hear this!" Scarlett turned up the volume again and waited as the news anchors chatted about the ball. Completely aggravated now, Scarlett wished they would just come to the point and deliver the actual news she needed to hear.

At last, the honey-skinned senior anchor turned back to the camera and said, "Anchorage is shocked at the news that its wealthiest resident, Henry Mitchell died suddenly last week, only hours before his beloved Iditarod began."

Liz groaned. "Why do they always make people seem better in death? Why can't they just say the man was a monster, and may he rot?"

"*Shh*, they're finally getting to the good part." The ball was shown on screen again, Scarlett in her deep purple gown held in young Henry's arms. *Disgusting*.

The anchor's voice carried over the footage. "Here we see Mitchell's grandson, also known as Henry, at last night's Miners and Trappers ball, dancing with an unknown fan of the sport."

"Unknown, really? How much work would it have taken to get your name—or your permission, for that matter?" Liz groaned, and her dog growled a matching sentiment.

Scarlett continued to watch and wait for more.

"It turns out his family wanted a few days' privacy before

bringing the news of Mitchell's death public, especially considering the unusual circumstances surrounding the bequeathal of his estate."

The other anchor—a short, blond-haired man—spoke next. "Well, I'm definitely intrigued. To tell us more about these unusual provisions, we have local reporter, Jan Rivers, on the scene. Jan?"

"I'm here, Rick," the reporter answered as a feed of her popped up onto the screen. She stood beside Scarlett's dance partner in downtown Anchorage. "Standing with me is Henry Mitchell, III, heir apparent to the Mitchell estate. Henry, is it true that you had no idea what your grandfather was planning?"

Henry shook his head so subtly, his chin barely quavered. "Not a clue," he said. "We were all surprised when—"

"What was he planning? Why can't they just tell us already?" Liz shrieked.

"Liz, seriously? I need to hear this!" Scarlett tried to turn the volume up, but it had already reached the maximum limit.

"So, you need to complete that list or you won't see a dime?" the reporter continued, making Scarlett desperate to know what she'd missed.

Both friends gasped and the line fell silent. Even Samson's barking had quieted as they all waited for the big reveal.

"Not even a penny, Jan," Henry answered confidently, a Cheshire grin spreading across his undeniably handsome face. Scarlett hated herself for even noticing.

"Now I've heard a lot about these bucket lists, but I've never seen one quite as ambitious as your granddad's."

Henry chuckled. "No, of course he wouldn't make it easy."

"I've also never heard," Jan continued, obviously reading from a prompter of sort, "of someone passing a bucket list onto others. I thought the whole point was to finish the list *before* you kicked the bucket."

"Well, Granddad didn't like to leave things undone. I know he always regretted not having been able to finish a race. Now he's decided I need to not only finish, but also place."

Both brushed straight past the myriad reasons as to why the cruel man had been banned from the sport, again eliciting a string of obscenities from Liz.

"A harrowing feat even for the most seasoned sledders. But it isn't just things he never did, is it? He also expects you to relive his greatest hits?"

"If that was a question," Henry said, locking eyes with the camera and sending a chill right through Scarlett. "Then the answer is *yes*."

The reporter continued on, making sure to hit all the pre-determined talking points of the interview. "In fact, you completed your first item off the list just yesterday. Can you tell us more about it?"

Henry stood even taller now and tucked a hand into his coat pocket. "Dance with a stranger the whole night without getting her name. Check and check."

"He used you!" Liz shouted.

Scarlett felt tired more than angry. "Are you really surprised, given who he is?" she mumbled while chewing on a pesky hangnail.

"That's not right," Liz said. "Get angry with me."

"Oh, I am. But what can we do?" She spit out the small piece of skin she'd torn from her finger.

"Don't dance with handsome strangers, I guess. Because they may turn out to be the devil in disguise."

"You said it," Scarlett agreed. "Lesson learned."

They both turned their attention back to the television. "Did you know you were being filmed?" the reporter continued.

Henry laughed. "Of course, I knew. That's a provision, too. I need to finish this bucket list and get adequate..." He made air quotes here. "...press coverage to help improve the stock value of Mitchell Enterprises. If I fail at even a single thing, nobody in my family will receive any inheritance."

"That seems a bit extreme. Why does this all fall on you?"

"Because he's my namesake, and I'm meant to carry on

his legacy. Granddad always wanted things to go a certain way. He hated failure, and—"

"Which is why he beat his dogs into a pulp!" Liz cried.

Scarlett couldn't argue here, it was all true—all so painfully true—and she'd let him put his hands on her. Deplorable!

"So, what happens to the money if *you* fail, Henry?" the reporter asked on behalf of all of them.

He nodded first to the reporter, then turned to speak straight into the camera.

Seeing his unforgettable eyes so close again sent chills straight to Scarlett's heart. His words then drove a dagger.

"It doesn't matter, because I will not fail. It's not in my blood."

CHAPTER 7

EIGHT DAYS LATER, SCARLETT AT LAST RECEIVED THE NEWS she'd been waiting for. Her best friend, Lauren, had finished her first Iditarod—and with a time of nine days, ten hours, thirty-six minutes, and twenty-two seconds. Although she didn't place among the top mushers, she was so close that people were already predicting a top ten finish for her in next year's race.

Scarlett's heart swelled with pride. Only the slightest pricks of envy marred her otherwise perfect joy at Lauren's accomplishment. Since both Lauren and the dogs would all need time to recover from the grueling 1,000-mile trek—and also to catch up with Shane—the two friends made plans to meet up over the weekend.

That gave Scarlett a few more days of brooding privately over having been used so heinously by a man she hated so thoroughly. Other than delivering the initial news, Liz was of no help. Instead, her oldest Alaskan friend only made her feel worse about the whole thing.

"How could you have danced with that man? How could you have looked at him like that? How could any part of you liked any part of him?" Liz had pelted her with question after question, and Scarlett didn't have answers for any of them.

On the one hand, Scarlett's Henry wasn't the actual animal abuser and slipshod businessman. He was the grandson of said man. On the other hand, didn't family have a way of defining who you were deep down inside? And the Henry she'd met at the ball had been arrogant and cocksure, just like his granddad. Could he possibly be cruel, too?

Scarlett wondered, but she in no way intended to find out. As far as she was concerned, Henry Mitchell, III was soon to be a distant—and hopefully forgotten—memory.

Good riddance to him and his asinine bucket list. Scarlett didn't even know people did that in real life. Yet another part of her once dance partner that felt as if it belonged in the fictional realm instead of in her actual flesh-and-blood world.

"What are you moping about this time?" The senior librarian, Mrs. Caputo, came over to where Scarlett stood mindlessly scanning books into the system and dropped a fresh stack of new arrivals in front of her with a thud.

Scarlett sighed and tried to put that night out of her

mind... again. Why was it so hard to forget something so unpleasant? Never matter, she had work to do, and a supervisor to please. She forced a grin. "Just catching up on the overnights."

"That should have been done already. You've been very distracted this past week. Is this because of that race?"

Mrs. Caputo was the last person Scarlett wanted to tell about the whole Henry Mitchell affair, so she simply agreed to the other woman's assessment of the situation. "My friend, Lauren... You met her once, actually. She ran this year, and I've just been thinking a lot about her."

The elderly woman nodded and looked down at Scarlett over the rims of her glasses. Such a stereotype, and one Scarlett loathed. "You've always seemed more concerned about those dog sleds than you are at your job."

Scarlett shook her head fiercely. Even though she didn't have much love for this particular coworker, she loved the work they did together. The last thing she needed was a reason to make her unhappy—invented or otherwise. "No, no, it's not like that at all. I mean, everyone has a hobby, right?"

The other woman snorted with clear derision. "But your collection is at least three steps beyond 'hobby.' Wouldn't you agree?"

Scarlett shrugged and took the first book off the stack

that Mrs. Caputo had delivered. She did not need this today. She already had enough to feel melancholy over.

The conversation took a surprise turn when the elder librarian cleared her throat and announced, "I think you should do it. Go hitch up some dogs and run that race."

Talk about a loop-de-loop! Mrs. Caputo rarely took interest in Scarlett beyond whether she was performing her job up to par. Why would she suddenly encourage Scarlett to pursue her dream?

"It's not that simple," she objected, hoping it came out kindly. "I'd need a team, practice, *lots* of practice. We'd have to run every day. It's a full-time commitment."

"It seems to me you're already committing your mind to it even when you're supposed to be focusing on other things." The woman made eyes toward the computer monitor and then shifted them back to Scarlett, who was reddening beneath her elder's gaze. She hated how much her embarrassment showed due to her pale hair and even paler skin.

"I'm sorry. I'll try to be better," she said, hoping it would be enough to get the other woman to leave her alone for the rest of the day.

"I think you need to quit." Mrs. Caputo delivered this blow flatly and without feeling.

"What?" Scarlett spat. She was great at her job, and she loved what she did, too. Why on earth would Mrs. Caputo be trying to fire her now? Did she even have the needed permissions to do so? After all, this was a government job and came with certain protections. Daydreaming could hardly be against the rules.

Mrs. Caputo picked up a pencil and began to scroll down some kind of list she'd brought with her. She spoke to Scarlett without removing her eyes from the paper. "Well, really more like take a leave of absence."

It took everything Scarlett had to make her face neutral again. She feared that anything she said in this situation would be the wrong thing.

"Thank you for the suggestion, but—"

"It's not a suggestion. It's an offer."

"I don't think I understand."

"As I'm sure you know, and are probably even counting the days, I'll be retiring in June of next year." Scarlett knew this well; it was four-hundred and sixty-three days until she'd be free of the old biddy.

Her colleague seemed to wait for some kind of reaction, but Scarlett kept her face thankfully placid. She took a deep breath and continued, "So if you want to do this dog thing, this is probably your only chance. Once I've retired, I'll recommend you take my place as senior librarian. Haven't really got much of another choice, have I?"

Scarlett waited for her to say more. These long pauses

frustrated her but were a common habit of her elder coworker.

"I need to spell it out, then?" Mrs. Caputo sighed and clutched her stack of papers to her chest. "The budget is tight as is, and it's probably best to only have one staff member in training at a time. When I leave, you'll need to train to take my place…"

Scarlett didn't mention that she already did the same exact job as Mrs. Caputo, and regardless of what the other woman thought, she did it better and with more enthusiasm, too.

"…And we'll need to train someone to take your place as well. If you take unpaid leave, I can train the new librarian in your absence, you can run that race you're obsessed with and, in a year, we can both move on to the next thing. It's really quite a good plan, if I do say so myself." Mrs. Caputo chuckled, a sound Scarlett rarely heard. When she did, though, it reminded her of a chicken.

Cluck, cluck, cluck.

Although Scarlett hated this, along with the proud look that glowed on the elder librarian's face, she had to agree. This was the big break she'd been waiting for without having realized it.

This was her chance to have it all—a chance to live out her wildest adventure and retain the security of her books waiting on standby.

As much as she didn't like playing into the other woman's hubris, she couldn't hide her excitement. "Are you sure, Mrs. Caputo? Are you sure that's allowed?"

"Why wouldn't it be? I'm the one who decides the staffing here."

Not specifically true since again they were a government-funded entity, but it seemed the woman had already taken all the necessary steps. How long had she been planning to oust Scarlett until she was safely retired? And was she doing this as a favor to Scarlett? Or, was it because she really hated her so much that she couldn't stand the thought of another year working in her company?

"I think I'd like to hear more," Scarlett acquiesced, and that hated look of condescension mixed with pride crossed her colleague's face once more.

"Wonderful. I'll bring it to the board. Now please get your mind out of the snow and back on your job."

Scarlett willed her tongue to remain still rather than help form all the choice words she had for Mrs. Caputo. If she kept her cool for a little while longer, she had the chance to do something truly special. Whatever her supervisor's intentions, the plan would ultimately benefit Scarlett.

And she'd be a fool to say no to this unexpected proposal.

CHAPTER 8

At last, the weekend came.

She needed her best friend now more than ever, and luckily she would finally see Lauren. After tucking a few new reading selections she knew her friend would enjoy into her purse, she pulled on her outdoor gear and began the long drive to Puffin Ridge.

The roads were sparse and well plowed, which thankfully kept Scarlett's old sedan on track. Alaskans often reprimanded her for not choosing a vehicle with all-wheel drive, but the truth was, she loved her little junker. Besides, a lower car payment meant she could spend more of her money on the things she enjoyed.

Hoping to catch Lolly Winston's newest song, she turned the knob on the radio and searched through the various stations for the familiar opening beats. A familiar voice, however, stopped her cold.

"—talking about my family's legacy here. I can't afford to fail, and I'm not used to it, either," Henry Mitchell, III's self-assured baritone slithered out from the speakers.

Scarlett jumped in her seat as her tires lost traction and spun the car around. Luckily, there were no other vehicles around as she wrestled with her steering wheel to regain control of the car. With a practiced swerve into the spin, she corrected her course, then returned her attention to the radio.

A local on-air personality, whom she recognized but couldn't name from memory, interviewed Henry for his show. "Surely you must understand that some people devote their lives to the race and never place in the top ten. How do you expect to do it in less than a year's time and with no training to date?"

Henry chuckled. "I don't expect to. *I will*. You'll see."

"We'll see, indeed." The host switched to his projection voice with hardly a pause. "Next up, we'll be talking to Henry about some of the items he's already checked off this infamous bucket list, including one shocking adventure that actually landed him in jail. But first, a word from our sponsor."

Scarlett slammed the dial, and the little car jerked again. She would drive the rest of the way in silence.

…Except her thoughts refused to quiet down.

How had Henry landed in jail, and why was he out now? She had to admit, she liked the thought of him locked behind bars. What kind of person did that make her?

A good person, she told herself. This whole thing had made her realize that now more than ever. If there were evil people in this world, then surely there had to be good, too. Scarlett always did her best to be good, so long as she had all the information to make an informed decision.

Once again, she chided herself for not first getting Henry's name before agreeing to that dance. Would she have instantly made the connection? Would she have danced just to be polite, or would she have told him right then and there what she thought of him and his family?

As much as she never wanted to see the man again, a part of her wished he *was* here with her right now. She'd definitely give him a piece of her mind, make him answer for using her the way he did.

He couldn't just get whatever he wanted simply because he was born into a powerful family. Too many people worked too hard, gave too much for him to just waltz in and take it from them like some reverse Robin Hood.

And now he thought—nay, claimed—he was going to place among the top racers in the Iditarod. Besides being ridiculous, it was also infuriating. Just as she'd refused his kiss, Scarlett also refused to let him sully the sport that meant so much to her.

She would stop him herself if she had to.

She would take that year off. She would assemble a team. She would train with everything she had, every minute of every day.

She would win that race.

CHAPTER 9

"I THINK IT'S A GREAT IDEA," LAUREN SAID AS SHE SAT IN HER favorite arm chair and patted her favorite dog's head. Briar Rose, a red husky that had originally belonged to Shane's daughter, Rosie, panted her pleasure. She had clearly missed her new dog mama while she and the team were out running the Iditarod.

Shane nodded. "Ever since Lauren finished a few days ago, we've been discussing the need to bring on some part-time help to work with the dogs."

"Now that I'm one to watch..." Lauren giggled as if she couldn't believe it. "Well, we need to ramp up the dogs' training schedule."

Scarlett's head bobbed back and forth between the couple. She loved how they finished each other's sentences now, when they could hardly agree on anything less than two years ago. Married life suited them.

"And I can't push myself any harder than I already do," Shane added, motioning with his chin toward the cane that lay against his armrest. The former champion would never be able to race again despite a grueling rehabilitation. He was lucky to be able to walk, and even luckier that his injury had brought Lauren into his and the dogs' lives.

Lauren turned to face her husband, an apologetic expression on her face that immediately worried Scarlett. "And I may have kind of, sort of told Oscar that we could board some of the rescue dogs here. We'll need even more help to make sure they're all taken care of."

Scarlett hadn't had the pleasure of meeting Oscar Rockwell for more than a few minutes here and there at official race events, but she knew his work well. He and his wife, Lolly Winston, one of country music's fastest rising stars, had started the Sled Dog Rescue Organization a few years back to help discarded and neglected dogs find a second life with their new forever families. In fact, it was their organization that had brought Lauren to Shane in the first place.

"Why are you looking at me like that?" Shane teased. "You know I would have done the exact same thing myself."

"I know," Lauren responded. "But I should have asked first before making the decision."

"*Umm*, guys?" Scarlett interjected. "Do you honestly

need me here, or are you just saying that? I don't want to impose, especially with you being newlyweds and all that."

Lauren stood up from her chair, thumping the footrest into place. Briar Rose trotted alongside her as Lauren rushed over and gave Scarlett a huge, constricting hug.

"Of course, we do!" she said with a huge grin. "And even if we didn't, I'd still find a way to make it work. You're my best friend, Scar, and I'm so happy we'll be spending so much time together!"

Scarlett hugged her friend back and squealed. Lauren joined her, and even Briar Rose let out a happy howl. Shane groaned but then laughed, too.

"You'll stay in my old room, obviously," Lauren continued. "You know, the white one? And you'll have to wake up really early each day, and you'll definitely have to bring me lots of books when you move in. That's non-negotiable." She turned toward her husband and wagged her finger at him. "And no ridiculous house rules from you this time, Mr. Ramsey."

"Yes, Mrs. Ramsey." Scarlett could see the love that shone in Shane's eyes. After such a hard turn, he deserved Lauren, who glanced back at him with the same sparkling joy in her smile.

"Oh, Scarlett, I'm so happy for you!" Lauren squealed. "You deserve this more than anyone I've ever known. You deserve your dream, and to have your job right there and waiting for you a whole year later? That's like a Christmas miracle!"

"Hun, it's March." Shane reached for his cane and moved his footrest into the locked position but didn't stand.

"So Christmas miracles can't happen outside of December?" Lauren demanded, pouting her lip rather ineffectually.

Scarlett laughed. She always felt most like herself in the company of her friends, and especially Lauren.

Now more than ever, she knew she was on the right path. And she knew that maybe—just maybe—she could actually harness her dream and ride it to the stars.

CHAPTER 10

AFTER MAKING A PLAN WITH LAUREN AND SHANE, SCARLETT gave official notice of her sabbatical to Mrs. Caputo at the library.

"Glad you saw the wisdom in my plan," the elder woman clucked. Scarlett practically expected her to start preening the feathers of her swollen ego, and thanked the heavens she would only have to deal with her a few days longer.

Finding a subletter was easy, too. After all, she had prime access to the librarian bulletin board and made sure to post her announcement smack dab in the center on a brightly colored flyer. She even managed to sneak an announcement onto the library's website without attracting Mrs. Caputo's notice.

Everything fell into place, and a couple short weeks later, Scarlett arrived with her trunk full of clothes, books, and other cherished belongings, ready to move in and become the Ramseys' new handler.

"You're here! You're here!" Lauren squealed as she rushed to hug both Liz and Scarlett, who'd only just come through the door.

"Special delivery," Liz quipped. "I expect you to take good care of my Scar-Scar while she's so *far, far* away from home."

Scarlett moaned at the tacky joke. "Aww, c'mon, Liz. It's only a couple of hours."

Liz frowned and tucked a stray curl behind her ear. "Still, I've been seeing less and less of you lately. Don't be a stranger, okay?"

"Never." Scarlett smiled to reassure her friend. She hadn't seen much of Liz since the ball, and that wasn't entirely accidental. Sure, she was busy preparing for her big move, but she also blamed Liz in part for what had happened at the ball. If only she hadn't canceled so last minute... Scarlett hated that she felt this way, but still couldn't help her emotions.

"Will you stay for dinner, Liz?" Lauren asked, closing the door to shut out the cold wind that had followed them into the cabin.

It was strange for Scarlett to see her two friends together. While on the surface they seemed to have much in common, they'd never really hung out together. Scarlett was always with one or the other, but rarely with both. Of course, it didn't help that Lauren now devoted her life to dog-sledding, while Liz preferred to stay as far away from the sport as possible... with an occasional exception for its more glamorous events.

"Can't stay that long, I'm afraid," Liz answered, shaking her head and looking down at her boots. "My father will forget to eat if I'm not there to feed him."

"Mine was the same way," Lauren said wistfully. Her own father had died suddenly in a car crash a couple years ago, which had prompted her to move to Alaska, hoping to uncover the answers to his long-kept secrets. "Please come out sometime and bring Ben with you."

Scarlett left the two to talk while she wheeled her biggest suitcase into the place that would serve as her bedroom for the next year. Funny how domestic and grown-up her two friends seemed, when she herself was reliving her transient college days, complete with a sparsely decorated dorm-like room and all.

Lauren and Liz appeared a few moments later, each carrying an over-full box of books in her arms.

"What have you got in here?" Liz grumbled. "Bricks and mortar?"

"Well, half a bookstore at least." Scarlett rushed to relieve Liz of the box. As the only one who never mushed, she was the least in shape of the three. Her Akita, Samson, kept her trim and made her a good runner, but lucky for her, the giant dog didn't pull on the leash hard enough to really test her muscles.

"I know it's pretty plain in here still," Lauren said, setting her box onto the empty surface of the nearby honey-colored desk. "But we figured you could decorate it however you want. Maybe we could head into town and pick up some paint this weekend. What do you think?"

"I think that sounds perfect," Scarlett answered, knowing immediately that she would paint the room a soothing sky blue—just like her room back home in Texas. She missed her parents, but she knew, now more than ever before, that she was in the right place.

"Oscar called," Lauren continued. "He'll be by in a few days with the new dogs. Wanted to give you some time to settle in first."

"Oscar Rockwell?" Liz asked with a raised eyebrow.

"The one and only." Lauren raised an eyebrow right back at her, as if the two had been bantering together for years. Scarlett liked that, even if she was still secretly mad at Liz.

"And will Lolly Winston be coming, too?"

Lauren smiled and lowered her voice as if confiding a secret. "You know I didn't ask, but—"

"Oh, could you?" Liz's fangirl was showing for all to see.

"Maybe you and Ben will be coming for dinner sooner than you thought," Lauren guessed with a laugh. "I'll see if

Lolly can come, and if she does, you are both invited. We'll make it an evening. Sound good?"

Scarlett watched as Liz gave Lauren a huge hug. Just as books and sledding had first brought Lauren and Scarlett together, music was now uniting the two of them.

Maybe they had something in common after all.

"I have an advance copy of her next album," Lauren said, kicking a foot at the worn carpet beneath them. "Want to listen?"

"Umm, yes!" Liz cried. "You've got this, right, Scarlett?"

Scarlett laughed. "Listen to it in here so I have some music to unpack to."

Lauren stopped short on her way out the door. "But what about your dad's dinner?"

"Missing it one night out of the week won't hurt him," Liz said as the three of them scampered their way back outside to get more boxes.

This was the beginning of something big, but just how big, Scarlett couldn't even begin to imagine.

CHAPTER 11

Scarlett awoke to an unfamiliar view. After a few moments of initial confusion, she jumped out of bed with more than her normal amount of enthusiasm for the new day.

She dressed quickly, throwing on several layers and three pairs of socks. Unaccustomed to the bulky clothing, she lumbered out of the house like a purple and green Stay-Puft Marshmallow creature.

Outside, Lauren stood waiting in jeans and a big jacket with unlaced boots to match. She was already making her rounds with the dogs. When she looked up and saw Scarlett, she couldn't hide her laughter.

Not that she tried, though.

Already starting to sweat after less than a minute outdoors, Scarlett waddled down to where her friend now sat on the snow laughing while one of the dogs licked her face.

"Oh, my gosh! What are you wearing?"

"Too much?" Scarlett did a little twirl. It was not graceful.

"Well, it looks...warm?" Lauren said as she struggled to catch her breath. "Yes, it's too much. I mean, c'mon, it's almost 30 degrees out here. That's practically shorts weather."

"Oh yeah, like you're such an Alaskan already," Scarlett said, bumping Lauren with an over-fluffed hip.

"Oh, girly. Just you wait! A thousand miles on the back of one of these sleds and you'll want to relish in all the warm weather, too." Something nostalgic flashed through Lauren's bright eyes, and Scarlett wondered what untold memory was playing on the private screen of her friend's mind.

Lauren shook her head and stood back up. "Tell you what—let's make a game of this. We're going to go through all the regular duties of a handler and if you can make it through without removing a single layer, I'll eat slurry for breakfast tomorrow."

"And if I don't?"

"Then you have to eat it."

"That's gross." Scarlett stuck out her tongue, practically able to taste the mushy dog food already. "I like it."

"So it's a deal then?" Lauren removed her hat just to really show off.

"Yup. Prepare to taste dog breath!"

"Oh, you think so?" Lauren laughed and led Scarlett to the supply shed. "First we have to feed the dogs, you guessed it, slurry. Difference is they actually want to eat this stuff. Sink's in the corner. Go fill up, buttercup."

Lauren patiently explained everything they did, and Scarlett listened intently despite sweating bullets.

"Now, we just ran through the icy tundra to Nome, so the dogs aren't going for any real runs yet, but we can't let them sit on their tails and get frostbite on their butts."

"Okay," Scarlett said, now panting like one of the dogs. "So what are we doing?"

"We're going to harness them up and give them a nice, easy walk."

"Why does that sound more ominous than it sounds?"

Lauren smiled so wide that Scarlett could see every one of her teeth. She looked crazy, and it didn't take long for Scarlett to find out why.

In a few short moments, Scarlett found herself holding a leash behind Fred, who was almost the size of Liz's Samson. Lauren stood at the top of a short hill with a small bowl of the slurry mix.

"I don't understand what we're doing." Scarlett shouted

up to her friend. "Is this normal handler stuff, or are you just being a butt?"

Lauren laughed menacingly. "Do you have a grip on Fred?"

"Well, yes, but—"

"*Hike! Hike! Hike!*" Lauren shouted into the valley.

In an instant, Scarlett's feet left the ground as Fred took off up the hill. She felt like an oversized kite as she struggled to get her feet back under herself.

By the time she finally found her footing, Fred was noisily slurping at his bowl.

"All right, great first go, Scar." Lauren snorted in an attempt to hold in her laughter. "Once he finishes his food, run him around the fence line and back to his hut. See you in a few seconds."

"Where are you going?" she asked as her friend jogged back down the hill.

"To get the next dog." Lauren called up over her shoulder, not even slightly short on breath. Meanwhile Scarlett had lost her breath from the heat alone. Still, she refused to lose their bet. Seeing Lauren eat dog food after today's torment would be especially sweet.

"Okay, it's official," she said later between breaths once all the dogs had run up the hill. "I now, officially, hate you."

"Aww, c'mon now, I only had you do one at a time. And I helped. It's better than I got on my first day. Besides," she said, gesturing to Scarlett's jacket on the ground near one of the food buckets. "I *really* wanted to win the bet."

"What? No fair!" Scarlett hadn't even remembered taking it off.

"Just getting you ready. I doubt Henry Whatever the Turd will play fair on the trail and I want to make sure you kick his butt."

Scarlett groaned and picked up her discarded coat, struggling back into the sleeves.

Lauren winked. "You don't really have to eat dog food, Scar. I may be mean, but I'm not a monster."

"Yeah, yeah. So what's next?"

"We're going to fulfill your dream. Darling, we're building your sled," Lauren said as she led the way back to her *she-shed*.

She opened the door with a flourish, revealing a bare-bones wooden sled.

"Technically, this was Shane's old sled. He had practically buried it under a heap of junk. But it was the one he started with, and I figured since we're training you to be a champion, you'll need a champion's sled."

Scarlett waved her hands in front of her face, trying to keep the tears at bay. "It's too much, I can't—"

"Nonsense. You can, and you will. Otherwise, you'll eat dog food, Miss!"

Both women laughed and hugged.

When they pulled apart, Lauren looked back toward Scarlett's new old sled and said, "We're rebuilding this not just so you have a sled to use, but so you understand how your sled feels and moves. Now get over here and step onto these skids."

A smile spread across her face and she hopped up onto skids.

"How does that feel, Miss Scarlett Cole-Hara?" Lauren often teased her about her namesake, combining her last name with the heroine's from *Gone with the Wind* as she did now.

"Frankly, my dear..." Scarlett started responding with her line, then sighed complacently. This moment was too wonderful to be lost in silliness. "It feels perfect," she finished after a deep, satisfied exhale. "Thank you for making all my dreams come true."

"One good turn deserves another." Lauren wrapped an arm over Scarlett's shoulders and hugged her again. "Now that I'm living my dream, I need my BFF to join me in hers."

CHAPTER 12

AFTER A BIT MORE TIME EXAMINING HER NEW SLED, Scarlett set to putting the remaining equipment away. Lauren had already gone back inside to help Shane with his early afternoon exercises.

That left Scarlett on her own, and she chose to spend that time studying the layout of the storage shed, to commit as much of it to memory as she possibly could. Athletic skill and building a stronger rapport with the dogs would take time, but she could study all the informational knowledge now—master that so she was ready when the other pieces of her training caught up.

The shed smelled of fresh paint and plaster, even though it had been completed while Lauren was out running the Iditarod as a celebratory gift from Shane to her and the dogs.

Where the chic new supply shed stood, a shabby, old

wooden one had once sat in its place. Shane had kept the doors locked firmly until the night he forgot to turn off a space heater and the entire thing took to flame.

Now it was Lauren's oasis and soon-to-be Scarlett's, too. Half of the space held neatly put-together shelves and well-organized equipment, and the other half hosted a couch, desk, and mini fridge.

"It's Lauren's new *she-shed!*" Shane had declared proudly upon showing off the construction that was more than double the size of its predecessor. "I read about them on Buzzfeed. It's her own little home away from home."

Lauren had kissed his cheek and said, "My home less than twenty feet away from home, and I love it!"

She had, of course, then told Scarlett she could use the space whenever she needed a little more privacy than her bedroom provided. The only stipulation was that she not bring out a space heater, especially since the shed was already equipped with its own tiny heating system.

Scarlett now searched through the shelves, committing the location of each item to memory. If ever she needed a snow hook in a hurry, she'd get one from the bottom right of the shelf closest to the door. The dog's harnesses were arranged neatly at eye level on a series of brightly colored hooks.

The extra dog food could be found—

"Excuse me?" A familiar male voice floated into the shed,

interrupting Scarlett's assessment of her stock. She knew exactly who the voice belonged to, but not how it had reached her here. Had she accidentally turned on the radio or something?

But, no, the dangerous combination of honeysuckle and lavender had seeped into her safe space as well.

Which could only mean...

Slowly, she rose from her stooping position and turned toward the door, hoping, praying that somehow her eyes would tell a different story than the one her other senses insisted upon.

But, no, Henry Mitchell, III stood in the open doorframe, light illuminating him from behind, making it hard for Scarlett to discern his expression.

"So we meet again," he said smoothly, with the smallest hint of humor in his voice. Did he think the pain he'd put her through was funny? Because she certainly didn't.

"What do you want?" she managed, crossing her arms in front of her chest and holding back a giant sigh.

"I had no idea it was you that night," he admitted. "I hope Shane will forgive me for flirting with his missus, because I need your help. I need both of your help."

The words washed over Scarlett. So much to take in. She'd prepared what she would say to him should they ever meet again at least a hundred times, but now that he had come, she couldn't get any of them out.

"I'm not…" she started. How would she finish it? Not going to help you? Not Lauren, as you clearly think I am? Not going to forgive you? The possibilities stretched on almost as far as the snowy fields outside.

Henry took several confident strides toward her. He wore a placating expression as if dealing with a disobedient dog or a difficult child. Scarlett hated it, hated him, and especially hated that, despite her anger, her body still reacted to his devastatingly handsome face and physique.

Devastating like an earthquake or a hurricane.

A poison.

"Look, I just—"

"You just need to leave!" Lauren interrupted, charging in and startling them both.

"Who's this, Lauren?" Henry asked Scarlett.

"This is Lauren," Lauren answered. "And you need to leave my friend alone. You've done enough already."

"I came here to see you," he said, unfazed by the two sets of angry female eyes boring holes into his skull.

"Well, mission accomplished. You see me. Now get out," Lauren growled. Even her normally pretty features seemed wild in her rage.

Henry took two defiant steps forward and now stood only inches from Lauren.

Lauren didn't waste a second. Having already had the time to memorize the contents of her shed, she bent down swiftly and grabbed a snow hook from the lowest shelf just behind her.

"Okay..." Henry said, taking a firm step back in response. "Look, no need to get angry. I just came to hire you to help me train for the race. I'll pay you well and keep the press out of your hair."

Lauren raised the hook threateningly above her head, which had the desired effect.

"Jeez, all right! I'll take that as a no for now."

"It's a no forever. Get lost!"

Scarlett watched as Henry stumbled back out through the door, as Lauren filled its frame, patting the hook in her hand like an old-school musical gangster. She practically expected her friend to snap her fingers and break out into song.

Everyone else played their parts in this little performance, but not Scarlett. She had forgotten her lines, trapped in the blinding spotlight of Henry Mitchell, III's confident gaze.

There would be no encore performance for her. No second chance to get things right.

She'd flubbed it up.

Again.

CHAPTER 13

SCARLETT SANK DOWN ONTO THE SOFA AND BURIED HER FACE in her hands. She'd always been able to stick up for herself before. Why did the very sight of this man catch her so off guard, cause her to lose her voice?

Lauren's voice, however, came through strong as ever. "What a creep," she growled as she slammed the door behind the now departing Henry Mitchell, III.

The cushions on the couch sank beneath the added weight when her friend plunked down beside her.

"What happened?" Lauren asked, squeezing Scarlett's shoulder.

"You came in almost right after him." Scarlett sniffed and blinked up at the light stuck to the ceiling. If only it could blind her from the memories that swirled furiously around her brain now, the regrets.

"Well, it's a good thing I did. You looked terrified. Is there anything about that night at the ball you need to tell me?"

"No, it's not like that." Scarlett gasped in horror, realizing her friend assumed that Henry had done much more than ask for a kiss.

"Then what is it like?"

"I don't know," Scarlett admitted. "I'm so confused."

Lauren popped back to her feet and began to pace the small shed's interior, picking up steam with each step. "Then let me fill in a few details for you. Shane will be able to say more, but here's what *I* know."

Scarlett listened in silence as Lauren reminded her all the reasons why Henry Mitchell, III was no good, no way, no how. Her friend was right, and the more distance Scarlett had from the man, the more she agreed. It was only seeing him again that had caught her so off guard that had taken her anger and twisted it into something else.

But what? Scarlett honestly didn't know, and she doubted she ever would.

"Not to mention," Lauren continued as Scarlett realized her own internal monologue had drowned out some of Lauren's. "His grandfather is the most despicable human to ever walk this earth."

Scarlett chose not to mention all the many other bad men in history, because that was beside the point. The first

Henry Mitchell had done so much wrong in his long life, and now he'd employed his grandson as some kind of sick agent to continue his legacy of cruelty, even from the grave.

"What else do you think is in that will? In the bucket list?" Scarlett asked, suddenly needing to know, needing to understand what exactly was at stake and where they might run into him again. If she was prepared the next time, then...

"Who cares?" Lauren exploded. "If something is done with evil intent, how can any part of it be good? For all we know, he has his henchman murdering puppies and stealing tax dollars. And make no mistake about it, Scar, he's a henchman."

"I know, but..." Scarlett twisted her hands in her lap, unsure of what she meant to say.

"But what? Please don't tell me you have feelings for him. He used you, remember that?"

"No, no, of course not!" Scarlett's heart sank as she lied to her best friend for the first time. For as confused as Scarlett felt about the man who was the topic of their conversation, she had all kinds of feelings for him.

Anger.

Curiosity.

Attraction.

The list went on and on, but she needed to keep the details of it to herself.

Lauren had made her argument known, and Scarlett couldn't disagree with a single point.

So then, why did her mind still drift toward the memory of his hand on the small of her back, his breath playing at her ear, even his cocksure grin as he told the world what he needed, fully anticipating he'd get it?

Why couldn't Scarlett focus on only the anger as Lauren was now doing? Why did she still feel trapped beneath his gaze even now?

CHAPTER 14

SCARLETT SHOOK THE SNOW FROM HER BOOTS AT THE doorway, only realizing now how sore her muscles had become during the course of that morning's training workout.

"How was your first official day on the job?" Shane asked brightly as the two women joined him in the kitchen.

"I'd say it was a lot better than mine," Lauren said pointedly, glancing toward Scarlett with a look of clear disapproval. "Except for our end-of-day intruder."

"Oh, is that danged moose back?" Shane chuckled as he glanced out the window in search of Puffin Ridge's very own moose menace.

"I wish!" Lauren grumbled, pulling out a chair across from her husband and plopping into it before at last revealing, "Henry Mitchell paid us a visit today."

Shane's eyes shot back to Lauren as if drawn by a magnet. "Henry Mitchell? I thought he had finally kicked the bucket. His ghost better not be haunting my shed, or I'll have to burn it down a second time."

"This is serious, Shane. Scarlett—"

"Was just as surprised as you were," Scarlett finally spoke up, tired of Lauren fighting on her behalf... Or, maybe it was fighting *with* her. This time, Scarlett couldn't really tell.

Lauren rolled her eyes, unwilling to accept this. "You know who I mean. She danced with him at the Miners and Trappers Ball."

"Oh, you mean the heir." Shane frowned and laid his hands out flat on the table. "I guess that's a little better than a ghost, but not much."

"This is serious!" Lauren was a fierce opponent. When she was on Scarlett's side, the other guy didn't stand a chance. This time, it felt like Scarlett was the other guy, and she hated it. After all, she hadn't done a single thing wrong— and she definitely hadn't asked for all this attention from Henry Mitchell, III.

"I still can't believe you let that happen." Lauren continued her tirade as Shane listened more or less calmly. Finding his happily ever after with Lauren had done a lot to soothe his once intense temper. "Scarlett—"

"*Scarlett*—" She hated how her own name tasted on her

tongue. "—can make her own decisions. Now please stop. This is all ancient history, okay?"

"If that's so, then why did he come up here today?" Lauren demanded. Both Ramseys turned toward Scarlett, so many questions in their eyes.

Well, Scarlett didn't have the answers, and she was sick to tears of being asked. "I don't know, but it wasn't to see me. He thought I was you."

"Oh, that's right." Lauren laughed angrily. "Get this: he wanted us to train him. Can you believe that?"

Shane shook his head, and Scarlett couldn't tell if he was more angry or amused. "How could he possibly think…?"

"I know! It's insane. He's all over every news outlet in the state, claiming how he's going to win, to live out his grandfather's legacy."

"A legacy of cruelty," Shane added, looking out the window once again as if he wanted to make sure that his dogs were okay at even the thought of the Mitchells.

Lauren grew louder as Shane began to join the argument —the argument against Scarlett. "Exactly! To even think we'd want any part of that."

"Can we please just drop this?" Scarlett begged. "I didn't know who he was then. I didn't invite him up here today. I have literally done nothing wrong." She rarely used the word *literally* because she hated how much the word's meaning had been warped by her generation. She hoped that using it now would get her friends' attention, make them realize how serious she was about dropping the subject.

"You know," Shane said, as if Scarlett hadn't spoken at all, "more than two-hundred dogs were taken from his estate in that big raid of 1987. It's the largest non-puppy mill rescue in recorded history."

Scarlett debated leaving the room right then and there, but she knew that would only raise Lauren's suspicions even more. So, instead, she tried her best to shut them out as she pulled out her smart phone and began to scroll through her Instagram feed.

"I met him once, the grandfather," Shane said, struggling to his feet with the help of his cane.

"Oh, I didn't know that. What was it like?" Lauren placed a steadying hand on her husband's arm as he stumbled toward the fridge.

He took out a Dr. Pepper and tossed one to Lauren, too. He offered Scarlett a soda as well, but she shook her head. The last thing she wanted to do was encourage them to settle in and dig deeper into this conversation.

They all knew what Henry Mitchell was, so why did they need to keep rehashing it? To continue blaming Scarlett for dancing with him when she didn't even know who he was?

"Exactly like you'd expect," Shane answered after a long, slow drink. "He was rude, arrogant. He put on quite a show, but no one was buying tickets."

"Sounds just like the junior."

"The third," Scarlett corrected before she could stop herself. She shrugged, trying to play it off cool. "Junior would be the second Henry, his son. The third is the grandson."

Thankfully, Scarlett's slip seemed to at last break the spell that had ensnared her best friend for the better part of that afternoon.

Lauren laughed heartily. "Oh, Scar. You can take the girl out of the library, but you can never take the library out of the girl."

Scarlett saluted her friend and smiled. "And don't you forget it. Now, want to go through some of the books I brought for you?"

Her friend beamed, all traces of the recent rage dissipating right in front of Scarlett's face. "Darling, I thought you'd never ask."

I thought you'd never stop, Scarlett mentally added. She just hoped Lauren and Shane had both gotten the need to gossip about the Mitchells out of their systems, because she really didn't want to hear about—or *from*—Henry ever again.

CHAPTER 15

THE NEXT MORNING, SCARLETT WAS LEFT TO WORK THE dogs on her own. Lauren and Shane had an appointment in the city and insisted that Scarlett should call with any questions that popped up.

Lauren had wanted to help the first couple of hours before they had to leave, but Scarlett wanted to try a full day by herself. It was always easier to learn without the training wheels dragging behind. Not that she didn't enjoy working side by side with her best friend, but she craved the extra responsibility.

She'd put her job on hold to give this sledding thing a serious attempt, and—by golly—she was going to do it right.

A part of her also suspected she hadn't seen the last of Henry Mitchell, III, and she preferred to meet him alone, should she meet him at all. Lauren had gotten far too worked up yesterday, and Scarlett wasn't about to go asking for a repeat.

Sure enough, as she was tying her strongest wheel dogs, Fred and Wendy, to her newly rebuilt sled, a sleek, luxury car pulled into the drive.

She turned toward the sound of spitting ice and salt, just in time to see Henry slam the door of his Mercedes and begin his approach toward the kennels.

"Lauren isn't here," Scarlett called across the slope of land. Today she would not be silenced. Today she would speak her mind—and give Henry a piece of it.

"I'm not here for her," he said, raising his hand to wave. "I'm here for you."

"For me? You don't even know me."

"Ahh, well, that's not strictly true. I may not know your name. *Yet*," he added with a smile. It was the only authentic one she'd seen from him to date. Her heart tightened defensively as he closed the distance between them and offered his hand in greeting.

"But I plan to fix that now," he said cheerily. "Hello, I'm Henry."

She took his hand and gave it a single, firm shake—a warning. But was it meant to warn him off bothering her, or meant to tell her own heart that he had no place occupying it?

"And you are?" he prompted.

No, she would not give into him that easily. She needed more from him before he'd get anything from here. She glowered at him, unwilling to play into his game simply for the sake of being nice. "Why are you here?"

"To get your name." He placed both hands in his pockets, casual, confident, cocky as all get out.

"If that's all you came for, then you're going to be pretty disappointed." She turned her back to him and checked that the dogs' harnesses were taut against their backs.

Henry bent at the waist, trying to make eye contact with her stooped figure. "And to say I'm sorry."

She laughed and watched as the little puffs of her breath broke apart in the air.

"Not exactly the response I was expecting, but I guess it's better than getting attacked with a snow hook." He laughed, too—and it felt real, not like the practiced chortle she'd heard him make on his many news interviews.

"I think we got off on the wrong foot. You don't seem to have such a good impression of me." He laughed, this time self-deprecatingly, but Scarlett refused to join in.

"How could I?" she demanded as she rose to a standing position and faced him nose-to-nose. "Seeing how you act like the world belongs to you? Knowing who you are?"

He sighed, his confidence shaken for the first time in her presence. "That's where you're wrong. You know who my family is, but you don't know me from Adam."

"Whoever Adam is, I'm sure he's a nicer guy than you," she spat as she continued to examine her sled and prepare it for its next run. The work kept her mind focused, which is exactly what she needed to ignore the strange feelings that flooded her senses whenever Henry was near. She traced her way back around and stood on the rack, her stance ready.

Henry followed her as she circled the sled and placed a firm hand on one of the holds beside her own. "Maybe. But could you at least let me explain?"

She shook her head and looked away. "I don't owe you anything, and I doubt Lauren and Shane want you on their property. Besides, I have work to do."

"Then let me help you," he seemed to beg. But that was ridiculous. This rich, entitled boy had probably never wanted for a single thing in his entire life.

And Scarlett refused to give into him now. Rather than saying another word to this second-time trespasser, she yelled for the dogs to "hike!" The sled took off like a shot.

Less than a second later, something warm slammed into her from behind. In horror, she realized that Henry hadn't let go of the sled, but had instead used his hold on the grips to pull himself aboard.

"You didn't say no!" he shouted over the rushing wind.

CHAPTER 16

Scarlett jammed her elbow into Henry hard, but still he clung to the sled, his body covering hers part for part.

"What are you doing?" she cried. "Get off!"

"Not until you hear me out." He gripped her wrist above the glove, pushing up on her jacket so that his thumb brushed the small part of her now-exposed skin.

"If I listen to you, will you leave me alone?" she shouted, hoping the shrill sound of her voice would ring in his ears, give him even half the headache he had given her.

"*Yes.*"

Scarlett didn't say anything as she considered this.

"I promise," he said so softly she wasn't quite sure if she'd heard it all. His normal bluster had vanished, and he was now speaking with her like a human being instead of a show pony.

For once, they actually had privacy and she could be sure that no cameras were directed at them and no friends would barge in on their conversation.

Which meant Scarlett had three choices then.

She could turn the sled around and deliver him back to his car.

She could push him off and let him deal with the consequences of being stranded and injured.

Or she could hear him out.

"Please," Henry said, as if he somehow knew the options that were being passed over in her mind.

"I'm listening," she choked out at last.

His body pushed tighter into hers as he moved his chin to her shoulder, so she could more easily hear his words. Fire threatened to rent her body in two—passion, anger, and a special tingly feeling all in one.

Would she have agreed to hear him out if her body didn't react this way to him? Was she being superficial? Betraying her values by even agreeing to speak with him?

She pushed these questions back to the dark corners of her mind, to be examined and re-examined at a later date. For now, he was talking to her frankly. He was revealing more of his mystery, and she wanted to hear what he had to say—to learn how her mind and her body could disagree so whole-heartedly when it came to this one single, unremarkable man.

"I didn't know there were cameras. That night when I asked you to dance. I didn't know they were watching."

"You said you did in your interview."

"There's the truth, and then there's what you tell the press. They're usually not the same thing."

She expected him to laugh haughtily as he often did, but he remained serious, humble. A part of her understood his point, but it also called into question everything he had told her until now, everything he was about to reveal. If he could lie so easily, then why wouldn't he lie to her?

"I'm telling you the truth now," he said.

"I'm not sure I can trust you," she admitted boldly. "I'm not even sure who you are."

"I'm just a guy who couldn't take my eyes away from you, because I just couldn't believe how beautiful you were in that purple dress. I kept trying to find the perfect way to introduce myself, but nothing seemed good enough. And then you came over yourself." His words caressed her ear, and she half expected him to lean in to kiss her right there on the back of that speeding sled. She half wanted him to as well.

She leaned away from him, and the sled jerked from the movement, spoiling the moment as she'd intended.

When they were back on course, she said, "So now you're claiming to be shy? How can that be when I've never met someone so sure of himself in all his life?"

He turned his face away with a hiss, and the missing warmth of his breath against her neck made her shiver.

"There's who I have to be, and then there's who I really am."

"So, yet again, here you are admitting you're two-faced, then. Why would that change my mind about you? Just because you tell me I'm pretty, you think that's enough to justify your behavior? You tried to make me kiss you, said you knew what I wanted. But I make my own decisions. And you know what else? I'm the same person all the time."

His voice came out hoarse, cracked—as if a strangled cry was stuck in his throat. "I can tell, and I like that about you. I wish I could be that way, too."

"So why can't you?"

"You just don't get what it's like."

Slowly, she felt the shackles on her heart break off and fall behind them in the snow. He was opening up to her. Should she do the same? She still didn't know what she could offer Henry, but she could start by hearing what he'd come to say. Gently, she said, "Then tell me."

Henry's grip shifted on the holds as if the coming revelation was something he needed to ready himself for just as much as he did her. He cleared his throat, but it still came out hoarse. "My whole life I've been groomed by my family—to take over the business, to uphold our reputation, to do exactly what was expected of me, when it was expected. It's a lot of pressure."

"Then why did you? Why didn't you just tell them no?"

"I tried. In college, I declared Biology as my major. Wanted to be a doctor one day, to help make people better. Maybe save some lives. But a few weeks into the semester, I got called to the dean's office and was given my new schedule. Just like that. I called my parents, furious, but my dad was even madder. He yelled and yelled about responsibilities to the family, said I had to major in business or I couldn't go to college at all."

Scarlett could feel his pain as he shared this memory with her. She'd been so worried about achieving both her dreams that she never stopped to consider what it was like for those who couldn't even grasp one. Henry was living a dream, but it wasn't his. This wasn't what he wanted. Did that mean she'd been unfair to him? Did it mean that maybe her heart knew something her brain hadn't caught onto yet? She felt more confused than ever.

He waited for her to speak again, and at last she managed, "So you gave up?"

He chuckled, but she could tell it was forced, a light-hearted defense against a serious problem. "Hardly. I found little ways to rebel here and there, but then when my granddad got sick, everything changed."

Scarlett bristled at the mention of the old man. "He was an awful man."

"I don't disagree. I never liked him, never wanted to be like him. Until I had no choice."

These words made her feel guilty and disgusted all over again. Back and forth, back and forth went her feelings for Henry Mitchell, III. Where would the spinning wheel finally land? And would she place the right bet before it did? "How could you have no choice?"

"If I don't follow his will to the letter, my entire family will go broke. The lawyers have been over that thing a million times, and it is airtight."

"What happens to the money if it doesn't go to your family?"

"I don't know exactly where it will all go. Some will go to political funds, some to venture capital. None of it to charity and none of it to us."

This made Scarlett livid on his behalf. "But he can't just do that. It's ridiculous and cruel!"

Henry sounded resigned, as if he'd used up all his anger on this matter long ago and simply didn't have any left to give. "I know that, but I'm not surprised—not from him. He always had to have his own way despite what others needed."

"They say you're just like him."

Henry groaned. "I know what they say, and if you believe

them, then there's nothing more I can do." He shifted one of his hands to cover hers. It was a small gesture, but a shockingly intimate one in that moment. "But something tells me you can see who I really am."

"You hardly know me," she said, wishing she could turn to face him and see what truths his marbled eyes held.

He brought his lips close to her ear again as he spoke. "I was going to let you go. I was going to let you walk away. That night, we hadn't informed the media yet about granddad's death, but I knew what was coming—the ridiculous journey through that stupid list, the constant media attention. Why would I willingly bring anyone into that?"

"So you let me go."

"I didn't want to, but I'm not like him. I care about other people. I promise you. I never wanted to upset you. I never asked to be a Mitchell. I never asked for any of this."

Scarlett's heart broke for him. If you didn't feel wanted in your own family, then where in the world could you call home? Here was a homeless billionaire, asking her to see him for more than his reputation.

"I didn't get your name or number. I thought for sure I'd never see you again," he continued. "Until I showed up here looking for the Ramseys, and there you were. And I just knew that I found you again for a reason. Do you believe in fate, that the stars can align to bring two people together?"

"I don't know what I believe," she said, but even as she

looked out over the crisp white snow paving their way, the sloping land rising to meet them, the clear skies embracing it all, she knew exactly what she believed. She, too, knew Henry Mitchell, III had come into her life for a reason. She needed to say something that would matter. She needed him to know she understood even if no one else did.

"Scarlett."

"What?"

"You said you didn't get my name, so I'm giving it to you. It's Scarlett. My name is Scarlett."

CHAPTER 17

IT DIDN'T TAKE LONG TO FINISH THE DOG'S EXERCISE WITH the added weight of Henry on the sled, and soon they were back at the kennels, their journey together over.

"C'mon, Fred." Scarlett released her favorite dog, a Malamute who ran as a wheel dog for the team, from the harness and led him back over to his house. When she finished retying him, she turned to see Henry marching through the rows of houses as Wendy led him to her place.

She watched as he completed the task quickly and competently.

"You're kind of a natural at this," she admitted when Henry returned to her side.

"I love dogs," he said with a wistful glance back toward Wendy. "Once when I was little, maybe seven, I snuck out to granddad's kennels to play with his, and I was so shocked by the mess and how skinny and angry they all were. All I could do was stand there and cry until my mom came to bring me back inside."

"That must have been awful," she said, placing a consoling hand on his arm.

Henry nodded. "It was. I wanted to help, but I couldn't do a single thing for them. When I got a little older, I realized some people lived like that, too. Not tied up, per se, but hungry, tortured, angry. It's what made me want to be a doctor."

She recognized the passion in his voice. It was the same in hers whenever she talked about books or dog sledding. She couldn't imagine life without either. "You still could be," she pointed out, even though she knew it couldn't be that simple.

"No, my family has made that clear." He laughed and ran a gloved hand over his head. "You know, most parents want their kids to grow up to be doctors. Not mine."

"I had no idea."

"Nobody does, Scarlett." She loved how her name sounded coming from his mouth and was glad she had given it to him. "Nobody understands. They just see me as a rich brat. They look at me and they see *him*."

"I see you," she said, taking a step closer. "At least now I do." Like that first night at the ball, she wanted to kiss him now. But she knew it would only complicate both their lives further.

He took a step to the side as if he, too, were fighting the urge to press their lips together. "That means everything."

They needed to keep talking. Too extended a silence would either mean giving in to their urges, and they both knew they couldn't do that. She asked, "Why can't you be who you really are in your interviews?"

"You *know* why. If I botch this bucket list thing, then my entire family loses everything. I need the attention to get sponsors, to have a fighting chance of making it." He sighed and kicked his foot at a patch of ice beneath the snow.

"And then what?"

"I haven't gotten that far yet. I'm terrified of failing. And no one in the sledding community will touch me, not knowing what Granddad did. Lauren and Shane weren't the first I tried to hire, but no amount of money is enough, it seems."

She had no doubt. The sport community was a tight-knit one. If one turned him out, they all would. Not even Lauren's big heart was enough to give him the whisper of a chance. In fact, she seemed even more furious than the rest when she'd spotted him here, and...

Oh, no.

"Lauren and Shane will be home soon," she said, hoping

her panic wasn't obvious. "Maybe you could tell them what you told me. Maybe they can still help."

"No, I can't. I shouldn't even have told you, but I couldn't stand the thought of you hating me... of thinking I'm like him."

"Then you need to leave before they come back." She hated to send him away, but she knew they couldn't be caught together.

"I know. I hope when this is all over, maybe I can see you again?"

She looked away, back toward the dogs, unwilling to look him in the eyes as she lied. "Maybe."

"Goodbye, Scarlett." Henry looked like he wanted to say more, but he simply stuck his hands in his pockets and walked back toward his car.

"Goodbye," she whispered after him.

Scarlett stood still and watched as he moved away from her. The anchor that tied them together had returned, but this time, she didn't want it to break. She didn't want to be another in the long line of people who had let him down, who refused to give him a chance. She couldn't do anything about his family problems, but perhaps she could help him with this one small thing. Perhaps she could make a difference, after all.

"Wait!" she called across the valley.

Henry turned and waited as she jogged up to him.

"Give me your phone," she said, only slightly out of breath.

When he handed it over, she punched in a number before giving it back to him. "That's Ben Benjamin's number. He's a friend. I'll talk to him. He'll help you. You don't have to give up."

He nodded and something glistened in his mismatched eyes. She felt so much for him in that moment: pity, awe, admiration, maybe even the beginnings of love. Before she could stop herself, she wrapped him in a tight hug—a hug of friends but also so much more. Even though Henry had his own things to work out, she hoped they might meet again one day when the timing was better. Until then, at least he had abated her anger—and what a beautiful gift that was.

"Good luck," she said as they broke apart. "I'm rooting for you."

And now she was. She really was.

CHAPTER 18

Scarlett waved after Henry while he reversed back down the long driveway. As his face now grew smaller in her line of sight, she wondered if she'd ever see it again. Of course, there would be the standard race events, but he'd be Henry Mitchell, III posing and preening for the press—not her secret, sincere Henry.

The anger had dissipated, but guilt quickly seeped in to take its place. She wanted to see him again, but knew it would be a distraction from his goal, a goal that was obviously important enough for him to deny everything he wanted out of life in order to make his family happy. She also wanted to tell Lauren and Shane all that he divulged to her that day. It would certainly make her life easier if Lauren no longer harped on her about his appearance at the cabin that day.

But that wasn't what Henry wanted, and shouldn't he be allowed to have at least one thing in his life go the way he wanted?

It felt wrong to keep these secrets from her best friend, but she would hate to be the one who spoiled everything Henry was working toward with his bucket list quest. Would the press still care about him if they knew he had a kind heart underneath all that bluster? Or did they only like covering him so long as he was a controversial figure like his granddad?

Would the truth spoil everything?

And if Henry wasn't like his granddad, where did that leave the rest of his family? Were they cruel people, too? Or were they also good people given a bad lot?

It felt so strange to pity a billionaire family, but in that moment, she knew she'd been blessed in her humble upbringing. Poor Henry had to play a part every day in his life. It was a wonder he even still knew who he really was on the inside.

And he obviously had a caring heart. He'd taken the nearly two-hour drive from Anchorage to Puffin Ridge that day to help Scarlett understand, to help her let go of that anger. He hadn't asked for help, just to be heard. That made a true hero in her book, the kind a girl could easily fall in love with.

If the timing was right, which it isn't, she had to remind herself.

She and Henry each only had one chance at the great race, and they both had to give it everything they could. The matter was closed. It had to be.

With a strengthened resolve, Scarlett finished the dog's exercises, taking extra time to enjoy the time on her sled as it brought back memories of Henry's body pressed so closely to hers.

She was just finishing up for the day when Lauren and Shane returned from the city.

"We're back!" Lauren shouted the moment she'd stepped out from the car. "Did you miss us?"

"Always," Scarlett said with an innocent smile. Lauren didn't need to know. The time with Henry could be a private memory, one just for her.

"Well, put on your best party dress, because we've got company."

Scarlett searched the back seat of the car, but it was empty.

"Not now, but tonight," Shane clarified.

"Oh?" Scarlett asked, intrigued.

"The Rockwells are coming and bringing the new dogs from the SDRO with them," he answered.

"Yup, and I already called Liz to let her know. She and her dad are coming, too." Lauren beamed at this reveal, and

Scarlett wondered when her two friends had managed to exchange numbers.

"Isn't this exciting?" Lauren asked, grabbing Scarlett's hand and giving it a squeeze. "You finally get to meet Lolly Winston!"

Scarlett squealed and jumped up and down as she was expected to—and she was excited for that night. Though she knew her focus should be on meeting the country star whom Lauren had only met briefly herself, all Scarlett could think about was the fact Ben Benjamin would be coming, too. She could tell him about Henry.

And ask him to help.

CHAPTER 19

Scarlett helped carry in several overstuffed grocery bags while Lauren chatted on about their plans for that night.

"We're going to start with king crab legs and a kale salad. Then we'll have prime rib with herb-roasted fingerling potatoes, and for dessert..." Lauren's eyes flashed with mischief when she revealed, "You're making cherries jubilee."

"I am?" That last part shocked Scarlett so much, she couldn't even comment on the fact they'd be eating at least two separate meals that night. Lauren did have a way of overdoing things sometimes, but it was one of the things Scarlett appreciated most about her.

"Well, I mean, I'm making all the other courses, so yeah."

"But aren't cherries jubilee served flambé?" A vision of

flames danced in Scarlett's eyes as she pictured a possible disaster of epic proportions.

Lauren shrugged. "We'll keep the fire extinguisher nearby just in case. Now c'mon, we've got a lot to do and not a lot of time to do it."

"Not that I'm not excited, but I thought the Rockwells weren't coming up until next week. What changed?" Scarlett unpacked the grocery bags while Lauren went to preheat the oven.

"*Plans* changed. We ran into them in the city today, and since everyone was free for the night, we asked them over."

"But don't they need more time to get the dogs ready?"

"More than time, they need space. They're really happy about us taking the dogs in early, because it means they'll have open spaces and can take on more dogs in need. They've had to put rescues on hold for the last couple of weeks due to the surge in demand."

"Well, I'm glad we can help."

"Seriously, Scar, it's a huge help that you're here. I never would have been able to manage all these extras on my own. And since I had to hire someone, I'm glad it could be my best friend." She bumped Scarlett with her hip as they stood together at the counter prepping ingredients for the feast ahead.

"Am I supposed to take the pits out of the cherries?"

Scarlett asked, holding one of the small fruits up by its stem to examine it in the light.

"Oh, boy. We've got our work cut out for us tonight." Lauren chuckled as she pulled open a drawer and gave Scarlett a small knife. "Use this if you need it. Just get those pits out of there while preserving the fruit."

Scarlett scrunched up her face, looking down at the knife Lauren had just placed in front of her. "And do I take out the stems, too?"

Lauren rolled her eyes. "Yes, the stems, silly!"

"Okay, great. Where's the flame torch? I'm ready to do this thing!" Unable to keep up the act, Scarlett burst out laughing.

"Not funny, Scar! We have way too much work to do already. Don't be a chore yourself."

Scarlett forced a pout, but couldn't stop from laughing again.

Lauren grabbed a cherry and popped it in her mouth. Her eyes grew wide as the fruit disappeared behind her lips. "Want me to do the cherries jubilee?" she offered. "I can give you the salad instead."

"Nah, I'll be fine. Let's get to work."

"Oh, speaking of, how was your first day on your own with the dogs?" Lauren kept her eyes on the food while they worked, but her ears were fully focused on the conversation.

Scarlett choked down a lump in her throat. She couldn't tell Lauren that she hadn't been on her own, not without revealing Henry's secrets. "It was good," she answered slowly.

Lauren dropped a hunk of meat into a pan with a thud and began rubbing it all over with rock salt. "Are you sure? It sounds like you're maybe a little upset."

Scarlett laughed. "What? Me? No. Just trying to focus on this recipe for the cherries thing. I like working with the dogs. Fred's my favorite."

"I should've known you would pick the trouble-maker as your favorite. Why am I not surprised?"

Fred hadn't given Scarlett any trouble yet, but she didn't point that out. Instead, she decided to take the conversation in a different direction and maybe do a little investigating while she was at it. "How was it for you in the start?" she asked casually.

"Oh, it was terrible. I loved the dogs, but Shane was such a grump. I was always afraid I was going to say or do the wrong thing and set him off. You're also starting with a lot of know-how already. This all was totally alien to me."

"But you figured it out."

"Yes, I did."

"And Shane became... well, less grumpy."

Lauren laughed as she plucked the leaves from a tiny sprig of thyme. "Yes, he certainly did."

"When did you start to change your mind about him?"

"What do you mean?"

"Well, you said you were always afraid of setting him off, and now you're married, so..."

"Oh, that." Lauren laughed again, and Scarlett could see how truly happy her friend was in this new life she'd made for himself. "It was a gradual softening, I guess. We had to live together, to help each other. Once he started trusting me with his secrets, it was much easier to understand where he was coming from, and I guess letting it out helped him trust me more, too."

Scarlett nodded as her friend spoke. She knew all this already. She needed more. "So it wasn't any one thing? Any one conversation that turned things around?"

Lauren set down the herbs she'd been working on and turned to face Scarlett directly. "What aren't you telling me?"

"What? Nothing. I was just curious, is all."

"You know about me and Shane. Why are you asking all these questions today? This isn't about Hen—"

"No, no. Of course, not," Scarlett protested.

Lauren washed her hands at the sink, keeping her eyes on Scarlett the whole time and waiting for a confession that wouldn't come. As she dried her hands on a towel, she sighed and said, "Scarlett, you know he's not—"

Ding dong!

Saved by the bell, Scarlett thought with a tremendous

sense of relief. Hopefully the night would be distracting enough to make Lauren completely forget about the interrupted interrogation.

Scarlett had never been a good liar, and she had always been too curious for her own good.

CHAPTER 20

SCARLETT WAS TAKEN ABACK WHEN SHE STEPPED OUTSIDE TO see the new rescues. After getting to know Shane and Lauren's team, she thought she was familiar with huskies.

But these were... wrong.

Something about the dull look in their eyes, the thinness, and in some cases, the whimpering. Several had to be carried to the new area for the rescues, so Scarlett tried her best to push past the overwhelming feeling of sadness for these poor, mistreated dogs.

A part of her wondered if this was what Henry had seen at his grandfather's. Now, more than ever, she found herself hating the man that, even in death, had forced his grandson to be someone he wasn't. What kind of depraved person could actually treat these magnificent animals like this?

The dogs didn't bark. They didn't even growl. They

seemed to move like ghosts through the new area of the kennel. Scarlett struggled to hear what Lauren and Shane were saying about needing to keep the new dogs separate from the team, but she had a hard time focusing on the words when the dog she carried with her seemed about to collapse at even the slightest bit of wind.

"Hey, Scarlett, that one's going to need to be in the shed for a time," Lauren called out to her.

"*Hmm?*" she replied, finding herself drawn into the dog's gaze, a beautiful mismatched set of eyes. Just like Henry. "The shed?"

"Yeah, Oscar said she's pregnant and close to having her litter."

How could that be true? This dog barely had enough strength to support its own body, let alone others. "But she's so skinny!"

"Yeah..." A strange mix of anger and sorrow swirled in her friend's eyes, and Scarlett understood it exactly—because she was feeling the same thing herself.

Scarlett hugged the dog to her chest a bit tighter. "I'm going to call you Fantine," she whispered soothingly to the expectant mother. "She was also abandoned after getting pregnant, but you won't be alone like she was."

She arranged a nest of blankets for Fantine in the shed and placed a bowl of food and tepid water by the head of the weary dog.

The job was mostly done, but she knew the work was far from over. Everywhere she looked, she was reminded of the soldiers that had come back from war. The thousand-yard stare, listlessness, mindless pacing. These dogs had been through Hell.

"It hurts deep down to see them like this."

She jumped at the voice and turned, half expecting to find Henry there again, but instead she was greeted by Oscar Rockwell, who stood with glistening eyes, watching the dogs.

"Sorry," the SDRO head and veterinarian said, approaching Scarlett and Fantine. "I didn't mean to scare you. I just know how you feel. It's why our work is so important, and you're a part of that now."

"What happened to all of them?" Scarlett asked, freely letting tears fall.

"It varies from dog to dog, but there is always trauma, always needs not being met. Some of these were rescued from kennels that were overpopulated, some from kill shelters where they'd been abandoned when their owners gave up on them. There's a rash of them every year, like rabbits after Easter."

"They just look so..."

"Yeah. It's hard to find the words for it. Huskies are normally happy and playful, eager to work. These are, for lack of a better word, *broken*. The black and white guy over there? He was found under someone's porch in the valley. He had a broken leg and nearly lost his eye. We assume he got on the wrong side of a lynx. Before that, we have no idea where he came from or the rest of his story. Took three months before he finally started to open up. The mother you were helping—"

"Fantine."

"From *Les Miserables?*" He chuckled. "I suppose that fits. She was stuck in a kennel that was little more than a puppy mill. We couldn't find ownership paperwork for the area, so it was probably an illegal puppy farm, and when the money got tight or the police got too close, the people in charge just abandoned the whole thing. When we arrived, half the dogs were dead, still chained up. The rest were malnourished. A couple had injured themselves trying to escape."

Scarlett felt her stomach churn. "I think I'm going to be sick."

"I'm sorry. I'm being a horrible guest. I guess I've become too accustomed to what these dogs have been through."

"How do you deal with it?" she asked, not taking her eyes off Fantine as she spoke.

"By focusing on their future instead of their past. You know everyone has parts of their past they'd rather forget, some beyond their control. In those cases, you're left with two choices. You can dwell on it and never be free, or you can focus on making sure tomorrow is the best it can possibly be."

Scarlett nodded. The vision of Fantine's mismatched eyes merged with Henry's, and she wondered how she could have gotten things so wrong when it came to him.

"I'll protect you," she told the dog and hoped that somewhere Henry had heard her words, too.

CHAPTER 21

As much as Scarlett looked forward to meeting Lolly Winston, she just couldn't bring herself to leave Fantine. Not yet.

This dog had been abandoned and discarded all her life. She had nursed who knew how many puppies and had them all taken away without explanation. She'd been broken, and Scarlett wanted to be the one to finally put the pieces back together. To give this dog a happily ever after.

"Shane's asking if you're ready to go over the paperwork," Liz's father, Ben Benjamin, announced, stepping into the shed with Scarlett and Oscar.

"Are you going to be okay?" the veterinarian asked her.

"Yeah, we'll be fine," she answered, stroking Fantine between the ears and trying not to feel discouraged as the dog stared at her with hollow, frightened eyes.

"I can send you some books on caring for pregnant dogs and puppies. Would you like that?"

"The answer is always in a book," Scarlett said with a sad smile. "Thank you."

"We'll see you inside when you're ready." Oscar headed to the cabin, but Liz's father stayed behind.

"It's hard seeing them suffer," Mr. Benjamin said, and Scarlett realized then that this sight must be particularly hard for him.

"Liz's mom..." she started, not knowing how she planned to finish.

Ben dropped to his haunches and let Fantine smell his hand.

"It must have been so hard raising her on your own." She'd always known that Ben loved Liz more than anything, and she doubted things would have been any different if he hadn't lost his wife at the same time he welcomed his daughter into this world.

"Liz is a good kid, always has been. It was hardest not having a partner going through life. It's lonely not having that support, that friendship." If there were tears at this memory, they had long since dried up. A quarter of a century is a long time to miss someone. Scarlett's heart went out to the poor man.

But she didn't know what she could say. The loss of his wife in childbirth clearly still stung after all these years. How could it not? Scarlett had always felt sorry for Liz, for never having known her mother's love, never having had the chance to meet her.

A new compassion for Ben Benjamin took root. He'd loved and lost, lost everything. Was that really any better? It was impossible to say.

She hardly knew Henry but already felt as if she'd lost something important in not being able to pursue a relationship with him, not now. Ben must feel it one-million fold to have planned a life together, to have started living it, and then... to end up alone despite all that.

Tears sprung to her eyes again.

"It's Fantine," she said, not wanting to upset the man who she'd looked up to ever since they first met.

He nodded and gave her a quick hug. "I know."

"Did they go to jail? The people who did this to her?"

"I don't know, but we can ask Oscar."

"How could people...?"

He sighed and scratched the dog between her ears. "I don't think you or I could ever understand, and that's a blessed thing."

"Henry Mitchell, he did this to dogs." Scarlett turned angry at this realization. Had this cruel man ever laid a hand on his children? His grandchildren?

"He did," Ben said, and Scarlett wasn't sure which question he was answering.

"And he never got punished for it," she moaned.

Neither said anything as they watched the frail husky twitch her legs and whine in her sleep. Fantine was about to be a mother again and still having nursing dreams from her own puppyhood. What a sad juxtaposition.

As hard as it was to continue this conversation, Scarlett knew she might not get Mr. Benjamin alone again that night —and she had a promise to make good on. "What do you think about his grandson going for the Iditarod?"

If Ben was surprised by this question, he didn't show it. His answer, however, was rather unexpected. "Frankly, I feel bad for him."

Scarlett turned to him, hope filling her chest. Finally, somebody understood, and it was exactly the person who needed to—but she had to be sure before she could say any more. "What do you mean?"

"The hoops he has to jump through. The threat of losing everything if he doesn't complete some stupid list at his grandpa's bidding. Make no mistake, if he doesn't get that money, I don't doubt there will be hell to pay with his family and the business shareholders. I wonder if the grandfather did it on purpose, as a way of getting the last laugh."

"But why would he do that to his own family?"

Ben shrugged. "Why would he torture his dogs? Why would he do any of the horrible things he did? It's not for you or me to understand."

Scarlett sniffed. She wasn't sure whether she wanted her Henry to win his challenge so that he could move on with his life and finally be free, or if it would be better for him to fail and let that miserable old man down once and for all. "Do you think he can do it? Do you think he can finish the list like he says?"

"It would be a long shot for anyone, but without a proper coach, he hasn't got a snowball's chance in Florida."

This was her chance. She had to take it. "Would you be willing to help him?"

Ben blinked over at her. When he saw the serious look on her face, he answered, "If he asked me, sure. I'd be willing to give him a chance to prove himself rather than expecting him to pay for the sins of others. I was given a second chance long ago, and I wouldn't be here today if not for those willing to take a chance on me."

Scarlett wanted to ask him what he meant. She hadn't heard of any sordid past, but then again, maybe Liz didn't know anything had ever been less than peachy about her father's past. Had Mr. Benjamin made an accidental slip in conversation, or was he trying to confide something deeper in her now?

She had two choices then.

She chose to honor her promise to Henry.

"Will you call him?" she asked after quickly explaining their exchange earlier that day. She let him know that Henry wasn't a bad person but left it to her forbidden friend to share more if and when *he* wanted to divulge it. "Will you help give him a chance?"

Ben frowned. "I—"

"Dinner's ready," Lauren called, barging into the shed and cutting off Ben's answer before he could give it. "Chop, chop!" She clapped her hand and motioned for Ben and Scarlett to come back inside with her.

As they passed through the yard, Ben caught Scarlett's eye and gave her a quick nod.

Now Henry's fate was in his hands.

CHAPTER 22

DINNER WAS DIVINE, AND SCARLETT'S CHERRIES JUBILEE WERE a big hit, too.

"You've got to give me your recipes," Oscar said. "I'd love to surprise Lolly with a home-cooked meal when she comes home from a long tour."

"Don't you go with her?" Liz asked, cracking into another crab leg even though they'd already had dessert.

"Sometimes," Lolly answered, rubbing Oscar's shoulder and staring at him lovingly. "But our schedules don't always match up, and our work with the dogs is too important to put on hold."

"But you're Lolly Winston!" Liz argued.

"Yes, she is," Oscar said and gave his wife a kiss on the cheek.

"You know, I have a friend I'd like you to meet the next

time she is up in Anchorage," Lolly told Liz. "She's also a very enthusiastic music lover. Her name's Riley, and she's my future sister-in-law."

"Oh, my gosh!" Liz shouted. "Does that mean you consider me a friend now?"

"Of course, just as long as you maybe shout a little less?" She winked at Liz.

"Oh, I bet it's loud at your concerts. You probably have headaches all the time," Liz whisper-yelled. "I'll keep it down, I promise!" By the time she finished that sentence, Liz had made it back to full volume again.

Scarlett and Ben laughed at the crestfallen look on Liz's face when she realized her gaffe.

Oscar and Lolly took that opportunity to give each other a quick kiss, and Lauren and Shane held hands across the table, each wearing a huge smile. The sight of these happy couples made Scarlett's heart sting with longing once again. She'd always been content to be single. How could meeting one man change what she thought she wanted?

"How did you two meet?" she asked Lolly and Oscar.

"Oh, it's a long story." Lolly laughed. "But a good one."

Everyone listened as the two took turns revealing the case of mistaken identity that had led to love. When they got to the part of the story about starting the Sled Dog Rescue Organization, their light-hearted banter turned more somber.

"Timber changed everything for me," Lolly said. "I miss him every day, but I'm so happy we were able to make his final years happy."

"He's the patron dog of SDRO," Oscar added. "We have a picture of him in the office, and our logo is actually adapted from one of his pictures."

"Did you ever get another dog?" Liz asked.

"We don't have one dog now. We have hundreds. All the SDRO dogs are our babies. They all need our love, and we are all so grateful for your help."

Something flashed in Liz's eyes. "Hey, is your song 'Soft Heart' about Timber?" she practically shouted, too excited to give the moment the respect it deserved.

Lolly nodded. "That and many others. First I loved the dog, and then I loved the man that had given him to me."

"That sounds familiar," Lauren said, squeezing Shane's hand.

Scarlett couldn't help but wonder if the love of dogs would also bring her very own prince charming—if maybe it already had.

CHAPTER 23

Scarlett soon found the days blurring together as she fell into her new routine. She woke up early every morning to give Fantine a bit of extra attention and found herself sneaking out to the shed after dinner every night to read with her and give her little snacks from the food Lauren had cooked that evening.

Spring was slowly coming to Alaska as it did every year, although for Alaskans it was known as the big "Break Up." The packed snow that had covered the roads for the last several months now melted and shattered like miniature glaciers, turning everything a dirty, mucky brown and gray. It wouldn't be long until they needed to start using wheeled practice sleds and an ATV to run the dogs.

After a quick run around the property, Scarlett once more gravitated toward the shed. The moment she opened the door, she could tell something wasn't right. Fantine appeared to have shredded the towels and pillows that made up her bed and now stalked back and forth like a coyote on the hunt.

Panic seized Scarlett as she tried to make sense of the scene before her. She needed to do something, but what? If Fantine got too agitated, what would happen to the pup—

The puppies!

She raced into the shed, slipping on a small puddle of dog vomit on the floor as she went directly to her birthing book Oscar had lent her. After a few minutes of frantic page flipping and hurried reading, she determined that very soon the shed would house a whole family of husky pups. The last time Oscar had been out to the cabin, he'd given Fantine a thorough check up and shared his prediction that her litter would be five puppies in size.

Part of Scarlett felt she should call Lauren or Shane out to the shed. However, that thought quickly left her when she looked into Fantine's eyes and saw the fear reflecting back at her. Scarlett knew then she'd have to be the one to help the soon-to-be mother deliver her new pups into this world.

"It's okay, girl. I'm going to be here with you the whole time. Are you ready to meet your puppies?" Scarlett gently stroked the dog's head with light pressure and pulled out a copy of the same Victor Hugo masterpiece that had served as the dog's namesake. "Now, where did we leave off, Fantine?"

She started to read aloud the way she did every night, hoping that this familiarity would comfort the dog. A few hours later, Javert had been thwarted once more and five little blobs now squirmed around Fantine, fighting for the best nursing spots. Scarlett wasn't sure why, but something still seemed wrong. And she couldn't take any chances here. This was a matter of life and death, and Fantine needed her to be brave.

After a few minutes of the dog continuing to whine and Scarlett not able to do a single thing to comfort her, she tried calling Oscar. When he didn't pick up, she left a hasty message and then immediately called again.

"Please pick up, please pick up," she mumbled, but it was no use.

Whether Fantine lived or died would be up to her and her limited experience. Doing her best to keep her voice steady, she read the birthing book aloud, looking for answers and trying to comfort the dog both at the same time. After everything the dog had been through, it didn't seem fair to lose her when she finally had a safe home.

Fantine panted heavily between whines and Scarlett felt tears welling in her eyes. Just then, the dog made a small noise and collapsed into the whelping box, her breaths coming out slow and fitfully. Scarlett began to cry in earnest now. "No! You need to hang on, girl. Don't give up now." she breathed out between the sobs.

It wasn't fair.

How? How, after all of that?

She knelt down and hugged Fantine's head to her chest.

A tongue flicked out and licked some of her tears away. Scarlett looked down into Fantine's mismatched eyes. The husky weakly wagged her tail and pulled herself away from Scarlett. Circling around, the dog nudged a sixth puppy with her nose. It was the smallest of the litter and mostly reddish in color.

"Oh! You still had another puppy in there! How silly of me. You obviously couldn't have a litter without your little Cosette. But let's see here. Who are your other puppies? Obviously, this big guy here should be... Lenny. Lenny Small. Aww, and this little girl looks like a Molly Bloom. This little guy looks like a Sam to me. Yeah, Sam Spade. And this confused looking pup is Don Quixote. And his grey and white buddy is Yossarian. There we go, Fantine. A litter of literary littles."

She laughed, stroking the head of each puppy lightly as she whispered their names.

Love had saved the day, and she knew her relationship with the dogs would be forever changed.

CHAPTER 24

SCARLETT THOUGHT OF HENRY OFTEN, BUT SHE RARELY needed to wonder how he was doing. The local news stations loved him. He'd even had some national coverage, which meant that Scarlett couldn't go for long without seeing his face or hearing his voice.

She most liked the times when she managed to catch a segment without Lauren or Shane nearby. It gave her some alone time with Henry—or at least, as close to it as she could come.

Every time her friends spoke ill of Henry, Scarlett felt her grip on his secrets loosening. It was so hard to hear them put voice to all the thoughts she'd once harbored as well, all the thoughts that Henry constantly endured from others.

It wasn't fair to any of them. She knew that when Lauren and Shane found out the truth, they'd feel guilty for all the unkind things they had said against Henry. But it wasn't her place to set the record straight. Everyone else always told Henry what he had to do, and she refused to be one of them.

As she watched him on the television now, she saw through his carefully made-up facade. Where he claimed confidence, she could see the utter terror that belied his words. When he smiled and laughed, she knew it hurt him somewhere deep inside to do so. He was a prisoner of his grandfather's legacy, living out the old man's final wishes, though he never got the chance to pursue any of his own.

Not yet, anyway.

Scarlett often prayed that Henry would find peace one day. Happiness. Love.

He deserved all of it.

After all, what good were all the riches of this world if he had to lose his soul to secure them? Scarlett would rather be poor and happy any day of the week.

Thank goodness she had friends like Lauren and Shane to provide her with this opportunity for her now, and even crotchety old Mrs. Caputo at the library who had come up with the once-in-a-lifetime chance to reach for the stars while still hanging onto all the things she loved on the ground.

The interview with Henry ended and a commercial for laundry detergent took over the screen. She powered the TV off and thought back to what she had learned.

A whole lot of nothing.

Henry continued to give the carefully constructed soundbites, continued to play in to what the press wanted to hear, what they expected of him. He hadn't given any real information about how his training was going, how he was liking it, or *whom* he was working with.

She thought back to her conversation with Ben Benjamin. He also hadn't reached out to tell her whether Henry had ever gotten in touch, or vice versa.

And Scarlett needed to know. Somehow, knowing Henry was being looked after by Mr. Benjamin would tell her that he'd be all right, that he at least had someone in her corner.

After placing a call to the old home phone at the Benjamin residence, she waited as it rung out several times with no answer. She'd always found it funny that they had a land line at all. Sure, Ben was of an older generation, but he had a cell phone, too. Why hang on to the home number when they didn't really need it?

"Hello?" Liz answered just as Scarlett was about to give up.

She had to actively mask the disappointment in her voice. "Hey, girl!" she said far too enthusiastically. "How you doing?"

"Scarlett? What are you doing calling this number? Why

didn't you just text?" Liz was short of breath, presumably from running to get to the phone.

"I must have pushed the wrong button in my call history," Scarlett lied. The last thing she needed was a lecture about Henry Mitchell, III. She'd need to find another way to get in touch with Ben.

"Weird," Liz said as Samson barked in the background. Normally a well-behaved dog, Liz's Akita always threw a fit whenever they were on the phone. "Hey, so when can I come out to see the puppies? And, more importantly, when will you come to the city to visit me?"

"You miss me that much?"

"Of course, I do. *Anchorage* misses you, too."

"*Awww.* The entire city misses me?"

"How could it not? You belong here. Please tell me you'll come into town soon. There's a new bar and grill I really want to try out, and I want you to come with me."

"I'm sure we'll find the time soon," Scarlett answered dismissively, but Liz saw right through her.

"Scar-Scar, I mean it. It's like you ran away. I never see you anymore."

"You just saw me..." Scarlett counted back to the night they'd spent with Oscar and Lolly and Lauren's ridiculously huge feast of a dinner party.

"Three weeks ago... Okay, maybe it has been a long time... Tell you what," she continued. "There's a race at the

Tozier Track next week. Shane and Lauren weren't planning to enter, but maybe it's not too late for me to put a team together and go myself."

"Okay." Her friend sounded annoyed.

"Come and meet me there, and we'll go out afterward."

Liz's voice returned to its usual cheer. "You promise?"

"Of course I do. I miss you like crazy, too," Scarlett said, even though, in truth, she'd been far too busy in her new life to think about the one she'd left behind in Anchorage.

And every spare moment beyond all that, she thought of Henry.

CHAPTER 25

W HEN S CARLETT TOLD S HANE AND L AUREN HER INTENTIONS to run the Tozier Track race, they both lavished her with encouragement.

"Of course, you should do it! Why hadn't we thought about that?" Lauren asked her husband.

"We'll come with you and make sure everything goes off without a hitch," Shane offered. "Then you can go out with Liz after, and I'll get the dogs home. Sound good?"

"Sounds perfect," Scarlett said, giving them each hugs. "How did I get so lucky to have you two in my life?"

"Stop with the sentimental mush," Lauren scolded. "We're all about the other kind of mushing in this family. Now hike, girly! We've got some training to do."

Lauren drilled her friend extra hard in the coming days, and Scarlett was grateful for the challenge. If nothing else, she'd know that she had given this dream her absolute all. After that, well, it would be up to God, to fate, to whatever larger plan was laid out among the stars.

The day before she was set to run her first official race, Scarlett went out for a practice run with Shane in the basket. Although he wasn't her usual coach, he wanted to have the chance to observe her technique and offer any pointers Lauren might not have made yet. After all, he was the one who had the most experience of the three by far.

Plus, this race was even more peculiar than normal—it was going to be done on wheeled sleds. Scarlett laughed when she saw Shane next to the four-wheeled bike/sled monstrosity. "Let me guess, it's just like learning to ride a bike?"

"*Hardly*. Welcome to chariot racing," Shane joked as he gestured to the half painted collection of metal tubes. "Careful, this thing is practically an antique."

Scarlett didn't know whether to laugh or scream at the sight of the thing. "Please tell me this is like the regular sleds."

Shane shook his head. "'Afraid not. You're going to have more traction, a greater risk of flipping and, make no mistake, you're going to get dirty. Still, it's a hoot!"

She laughed at his comical expression. "A hoot? What are you, fifty? Wait a minute... Did you say greater risk of flipping?" She rubbed her shoulder reflexively, remembering a past injury from this very thing—a flipped sled.

"Don't worry. I brought helmets." He held up two bright pink bike helmets. "Sorry we don't have anything in your colors yet, but we hadn't even considered this race until you brought it up."

"*My* colors?" she asked as Shane slapped the helmet on top of her head and climbed into the chair at the front of the so-called chariot.

"You don't think that I was running my team with pink jacketed dogs before Lauren, do you? It's just a little something to give you an identity and give you pride in your racing. Now, let's see if this thing still holds together."

Scarlett smiled as she let off the brakes and yelled to the team. "Hike!"

The difference in this ride became immediately apparent. There were no shock absorbers in the rig, so they felt every bump full-on. The wheels dug in whenever the dirt was loose, and she had to throw her weight to the side to keep from flipping them to the ground. This couldn't be good for Shane and his weakened legs.

Still, if he was in pain, he didn't let on. He was all business now that he was in the coach's seat. "Basic principles are the same," he shouted, his voice taking on a funny, vibrato quality from the bumpy ride. "But you and the dogs work harder for it. After this race, you should probably continue training the dogs with the chariot a couple of times a week. It doesn't fully apply to sled work, but it will keep you in fighting form."

Scarlett nodded through clenched teeth and shouted to her leashed dogs as they came up on the turn. "Gee! Gee! Gee!" she yelled, commanding them to go right. The dogs turned as instructed, but the sled did not.

"Turn the handle bars!" Shane shouted.

Scarlett yanked at them sharply, and the rig rose up on two wheels. She jumped to the high side of the sled, and thankfully her weight slammed it back down to the ground. "You might've said something before!" she chastised Shane.

"Sorry, didn't think about it. It's been a long time."

She laughed and did her best old man impression. "Back in my day, we had to carry the dogs, uphill the whole way, barefoot while being chased by a moose."

They both laughed and continued to take jabs at each other as they finished Scarlett's first run with the chariot.

"Thanks for that, coach," she told Shane after returning the dogs to their kennels.

"No problem," Shane wheezed.

"You're hurt!" she cried, rushing to lend Shane a hand.

"I'll be fine. Besides, it was worth it. I've really enjoyed watching you and Lauren come into your own with the dogs," he said wistfully. "It lets me relive my own glory days."

"Do you miss it?"

"Constantly," he confessed. "But I've also found a different kind of fulfillment in helping the both of you. It's nice to just enjoy the sport without all the drama, you know?"

She found the cane and returned it to Shane, but stayed closed in case he needed extra help tracking his way back to the cabin. "Actually, I don't. You haven't told me much about your early days."

He laughed. "Haven't I? You know the basics. Evil ex-wife, disappointed family, the works. I had to give up a lot for my love of the sport. You and Lauren are both so lucky that you haven't, and that makes me happier than you could possibly imagine."

Scarlett knew about Shane's background as an oil baron. She knew about his evil ex Isabel, too. It was only now, though, that she realized how much he and Henry actually had in common.

"Can I tell you something?" she asked, needing to share with someone before her secrets ate her alive.

"You can tell me anything," Shane said with a concerned look taking over his eyes.

That concern grew when she said, "But you can't tell Lauren."

"Ouch, that will be a hard one."

"Please, Shane? I really need to get this off my chest, and

I promise I will tell Lauren as soon as I can. I just can't… not yet."

"Okay, I can see you're upset. Tell me what's going on."

They stopped walking and stood together in the snow.

"It's about Henry Mitchell, III," Scarlett said as soon as she was sure Lauren was nowhere near. "He came back after that day that Lauren chased him away with a snow hook, and we talked."

Shane nodded. "I suspected something was up, but didn't want to say anything. I can see the way you tense up whenever he comes on the screen, but I can also tell that it's not an angry tension. It's something else."

"You're too smart for your own good, Shane. You haven't said anything to Lauren about that, have you?"

"I didn't know for sure, and now you're telling me not to. So no, I haven't and I won't. But please never ask me to keep secrets from my wife again."

"I won't." She shook her head adamantly, then sighed. "Henry's not what people think he is, Shane. It's all his family. They're forcing him. He doesn't want any of this. He wants to be a doctor, not a celebrity businessman."

"He puts on a good show, doesn't he? He certainly had me fooled. Are you sure he wasn't lying to you when he said all this?"

"No, I know somehow deep down, I just know he's telling the truth. And I feel bad for him, Shane."

"Well, I can certainly understand where he's coming from, having been there to a lesser extent myself."

Her face searched his for an answer, but found none there. "So what can I do?"

"What do you mean what can you do? You have to respect his wishes."

"Even if it's not who he really is?"

He frowned and placed a hand on her shoulder in a paternal gesture. "Scarlett, let me tell you something important. Sometimes people are exactly what you think they are, but sometimes they're someone else entirely. Sometimes our families define us, and sometimes all they give us is a name. And what's in a name? It's just a word, a sound."

"Words have power," Scarlett whispered, believing that with every fiber of her being.

Shane nodded before saying, "But so do feelings. Trust what yours tell you, and let the rest of it be damned."

CHAPTER 26

Rocks pinged and tinked off the underside of the truck as they pulled into the race area. Scarlett watched out the window, hoping to catch a glimpse of Henry. Would he have opted to compete in this non-traditional race, too?

Sure enough, it didn't take long to find him, though he was hard to make out through the giant wall of cameras that flanked him in an arc. He talked and smiled while struggling to set up his sled under the watchful eye of Ben Benjamin and thousands of viewers alike.

Scarlett breathed a sigh of relief now that she finally knew firsthand that Ben had followed through on their conversation. Henry had a good man on his side. Perhaps that would be enough.

"Nervous?" Lauren said, patting her on the knee. "I'm sure you'll do better than I did here on my first race."

Scarlett blushed but tried to hide it as jitters. "Yeah, I was just saying to myself, I hope I don't flip the chariot."

"Chariot? Has Shane been trying to convince you to call that hunk of junk a chariot?"

"Guilty as charged," Shane called from the backseat. "I even offered to put those spiky things on the wheels to give her an edge if she had to pass someone, but she turned me down."

"You didn't!" Lauren acted scandalized.

"Nah, but I still put in the other James Bond-style gadgets. Remember, the red button is the ejector seat." Shane laughed.

Lauren rolled her eyes and pushed Scarlett away from Shane and the truck. "Let's get you checked in."

Scarlett glanced back as her friend led her away. "But what about the char—"

"I want Shane to get that thing down. I can't have you needing a tetanus shot before your first race," Lauren answered. "Speaking of things that make you sick..."

Scarlett followed her friend's gaze and found that it was glued right on Henry. She laughed nervously rather than say anything to chastise Henry or come to his defense.

"The sport deserves more attention, but I hate that it's coming like this," Lauren growled only part under her breath.

"Let's just get checked in."

"Yes, don't let him ruin your day. You've got this, girl."

Scarlett chose not to mention that seeing Henry close up like this was actually a bright spot in the day.

Lauren pushed through the reporters and strode up to Ben Benjamin while Scarlett stumbled behind. "Checking in the winning racer, Scarlett Cole," she projected so all the nearby members of the press could hear, too. "Write that in your articles!"

"Good luck out there today, Scarlett," Ben said as he made a check on his list. "This will be a fun one."

"I hope you're right."

"I'm always right. You'll see," he said with a wink. "Oh, Lauren, it looks like Shane may need a little help corralling the dogs." He motioned with his chin toward the parking lot where Shane struggled to hook up Fred.

"Oh, shoot! I told him not to... Grrr." Lauren pushed her way back through the reporters, leaving Scarlett alone with Ben, and also Henry, who continued to work nearby.

She had so much to say but knew it would all be picked up by the cameras and likely replayed ad nauseam. "Good luck today," she called to him.

He looked up, smiled, waved in a way that suggested he'd been keenly aware of her presence this whole time. Then the sincerity slipped away, and he said, "I don't need luck. Enjoy coming in second!"

A series of flashes followed as the press took their

pictures—probably overjoyed with this new rivalry angle for their stories.

Ben put an arm around her shoulder and turned her away from the media. "Liz is running late, but she told me she'd be here by the time you finish." He glanced toward Henry for a moment before adding, "And then from there, you can ride together to the Otter's Drop."

"Okay, got it," she answered before trotting over to help Shane and Lauren ready her team. Had Henry said something to Ben? Was he helping them conspire to meet? Would she see more of him later that day?

Unfortunately, she didn't have long to mull these questions over.

She had a race to win.

CHAPTER 27

SCARLETT FELT A RUSH EVEN BEFORE SHE'D STARTED MOVING. The chariot stood much higher off the ground than her usual sled, and she'd been able to wear a cute warm weather outfit instead of her usual layers upon layers to keep the cold out. Even with a light jacket on, she felt overdressed in the balmy fifty degree spring air. Yup, she'd definitely toughened up over the last month with Lauren and Shane. She was a real Alaskan now, and a real musher, too.

She waited as Ben Benjamin signaled the start for each individual team. The first to pull away hit a huge puddle directly, which shot a spray of mud toward the waiting teams.

Shane was right. This was going to get dirty.

Henry started before her, and she silently cursed her bad

luck. If he started before her, he'd probably finish before her and could very well be gone by the time she finished... So much for finally getting to talk to him again.

Before she had too much time to wallow in self-pity, Mr. Benjamin gave her the signal to start.

"Hike!" she cried, then hung on for dear life.

The team was in top form today, rushing the track like they'd been waiting for this forever and a day. She wondered if they still felt Nome in their bones, if they longed for another big race like the one Lauren had taken them on for the Iditarod.

Almost a mile into the track now, the dogs had become more mud than fur, happy little golems charging forth like Shakespeare's proverbial dogs of war. Scarlett hazarded a glance down at herself and found that she herself had become a mermaid of mud. What a sight they must be!

"Haw!" Scarlett called as they reached their first turn, then she whistled and clicked like a crazed bird.

Her wheel dogs were her favorites, and she knew just how to get them to perform for her. Wendy liked when she would occasionally say their name and click her tongue. Fred enjoyed a quick whistle. Seeing the bond Scarlett had formed with them already, Lauren had insisted Scarlett use them as the basis for creating her own team. She'd said she could easily pick two more dogs to balance her team, but Scarlett needed to find at least sixteen, which would be much harder.

If only Fantine and her puppies would be ready, that would be another seven right there. But the idea was ludicrous, of course. Fantine would never be strong enough, and her puppies needed more time to grow and train—along with some time to enjoy being puppies, of course. And Scarlett had already decided that, no matter what happened with her future as a musher, she'd be adopting both Fantine and her runt, Cosette, and giving them a forever home.

Her team continued to fly across the track, and soon another musher came into her sights ahead. Oh, this was new. How did she pass? She'd never done this before.

With all the practice and grace of a newborn moose, she held on harder and tried to remember the proper command for overtaking another sled. She had to figure it out fast, too.

"Umm, keep going?" she called, barely above a whisper.

Her Malamute Fred looked back, seemingly disappointed in her.

"I'm new, buddy, I don't remember what to say to get you guys to go on by the— *Right!* On by! On by!" she shouted out and was pleased when Fred pick up his pace. His pink flapping tongue hung out from the side of his mouth. She'd made him proud, or at least she liked to think so.

As they passed the other teamed, she glanced over to offer a friendly smile, only to see it was Henry who would soon be eating her dust... or rather mud.

"Fancy meeting you here," she called.

"Come here often?" he called back.

"Nooo." She laughed, almost losing her hold on the chariot as she did. "Whoah."

Her team responded to the unintentional command and began to slow.

"No, no, I didn't mean that!" she argued, but Henry was pulling ahead again.

"Faster, please?" she asked Fred. "Hike like you've never hiked before!"

The dogs complied, and it didn't take long for her to catch sight of Henry's team again.

This was it, the home stretch. Now it was just a matter of—

Clank.

Once again, Scarlett nearly fell from the chariot. Only this time, it wasn't an easy correction to stay onboard. Hazarding a glance behind her, she saw one of her wheels zooming off into the Alaskan wilderness on its own. She quickly jumped over to the side of the chariot that still had its hind wheel in place and tried to balance as best she could.

The finish line grew visible in the distance. They were so close. She could still finish this thing more or less in one piece.

Thwack!

The chariot hit a stray bit of branch that had fallen onto

the track. It was enough to toss her from her precarious position and into the mud below.

She sat there in her own personal puddle, completely shook and watching helplessly as her dogs forged on and finished the race without her.

CHAPTER 28

SCARLETT PRESSED HER HANDS DOWN INTO THE SQUISHY MUD and used them to pry herself back onto shaky feet. The finish line was just there. Her team had already crossed along with what was left of the rig. If she could cross, too, she'd have at least completed what she set out to do—even if she couldn't win.

A couple other teams passed her by as she ambled forward like a mud zombie. She was covered in the stuff. Even her white-blonde hair was caked in dark, sticky mud. She used the inside of her T-shirt sleeve to wipe at her eyes and kept moving toward that line and the bystanders who flanked it just beyond.

As soon as she crossed, she fell back to the earth in a tired heap. Everything hurt, but luckily nothing seemed broken—well, besides the chariot.

Liz rushed over and helped her back up. "Oh, my gosh, that was so awesome! You should have seen that wipe out. You were like a regular Indiana Jones back there!"

"I'm glad my pain could amuse you," Scarlett said with a cough.

Liz's face fell. "I didn't mean to—"

"Relax, I'm just teasing. It was pretty awesome driving that thing home with one wheel. It would have been perfect if I hadn't taken that spill."

"We're still going out to the Otter's Drop, right? Everyone says they have the best clam fritters."

"Like this?" Scarlett shrieked. When she looked down at herself, she only saw brown.

"Don't want to wear your battle wounds with pride, huh?" Liz teased even as she wrinkled her nose at the grotesque sight of Scarlett before her.

Scarlett felt half-tempted to saddle her with a big, old hug. "*Har har.* And what about my team?"

"Shane's already working on loading them up. He said to tell you something about not expecting you to actually *use* the ejector seat." She shrugged. "Whatever that means."

Scarlett would have to chide Shane later for that one and for sending her out on that death trap in the first place. You would think a man who almost lost his life on a sledding trip gone wrong would be a little more careful with these things. She took a deep breath. Some of the mud that had already begun to dry on her arms cracked and fell off. "Okay, so that settles the dogs, but I am not going out for a night on the town covered in mud."

"Yeah, you do kind of stink, and now you're shedding. *Eek! I* guess we could stop by my house to give you a quick shower first. "

"You're such a good friend," Scarlett teased. "I'll make sure to leave as much of this as possible behind in your car."

Liz's nose wrinkled again. "That's just one of the many reasons I have no desire to do this thing for myself. I've got some towels in the trunk. Hopefully they'll be enough. C'mon, let's get you cleaned up."

"But I want to find out who won first," Scarlett said, looking back toward the crowd whose attention was focused intently elsewhere.

"I can tell you who won. It was your *lover*, Henry Mitchell, the turd."

"Someone's been hanging out with Lauren, I see. And a kindergarten class," Scarlett spat back.

"Are you really going to make fun of me right now, poopy McGee?"

Scarlett groaned. "I guess I really don't have a leg to stand on, but still, it's good sportsmanship to congratulate the winner before we go."

"Are you serious right now? He's not a good sport, so why should you be? Besides, do you really want to be on camera like that?" Liz looked her up and down as if to remind Scarlett she was dressed in a sheath of mud.

"*Ugh*, you're right. Let's just get out of here."

"Finally!" Liz made to put an arm around Scarlett to help guide her back to the parking lot, but then seemed to think better of it. "*Umm*, you know the way."

As they departed, she looked back toward the crowd where Henry stood proudly on some kind of raised podium giving a victory speech. She didn't think she'd ever seen anyone treat any race—let alone such a small one—as an Oscars ceremony.

His eyes shifted away from his interviewers and toward Scarlett, or at least the mud monster that had taken her place. He nodded subtly, so subtly she couldn't be sure his face had moved at all.

Was he trying to tell her something? If so, what?

"C'mon, look alive!" Liz shouted, and Scarlett realized she'd stopped to stand in place, trapped under Henry's hot gaze once again.

With one last glance back his way, she forced her eyes toward the parking lot and toddled after Liz. Henry wasn't a love interest anymore, nor should he have ever been. He was a rival.

He was the one to beat if she had any hope of achieving this dream.

So why didn't it feel like any of that mattered?

CHAPTER 29

SCARLETT FOLLOWED LIZ INTO THE NEW OTTER'S DROP BAR & Grille shyly. Since her clothes were covered in dried-on mud, she'd needed to borrow an outfit from Liz. She *had* packed a change of clothes, but Liz didn't approve of the simple jeans and T-shirt she'd planned for the evening. Instead, Scarlett wore a skirt that showed off her knees and a top that showed off the beginnings of her modestly proportioned cleavage. At least the colors went well with the angry purple bruises that mottled her otherwise fair skin, especially on the side that had taken the brunt of her fall.

"I feel weird," she told her friend.

"But you look great, and that's what matters." Liz beamed at her, but Scarlett kept her eyes focused on the giant surge of people ahead.

"Look at this place, it's packed," she said.

"Well, yeah, it's a Saturday night! And, hey, I think I see a free table over there." Liz yanked her arm and led her toward the back of the restaurant to claim the newly freed table before anyone else could beat them to it.

"That was a lucky break!" She breathed out a giant whoosh of air as she slid into the booth.

"Don't say break," Scarlett said, rubbing her elbow, which still stung from the race.

"Sorry." Liz laughed. "But, man, I've missed you."

Scarlett raised an inquisitive eyebrow. "Aren't your other friends keeping you busy?"

"They're not like you, Scarlett. You're more like a sister than a friend, and I've missed you."

She groaned. "Stop being so sweet. Go back to making fun of me, please."

"I mean it!" Liz insisted. "I can't wait for you to come back to your old life."

Scarlett had avoided thinking about that as much as possible. What happened when the year was over and her leave had ended? Would she go back to her job and forget this whole year ever happened? Or would she choose to pursue racing full-time and give up her work at the library? Neither option seemed right, but she knew she couldn't have both together.

At least she still had plenty of time to figure things out.

"You look upset." Liz reached across the table and squeezed Scarlett's hand. "Did I say something wrong?"

"No, it's not like that. It's just..."

Scarlett hadn't known how she planned to finish that sentence, but luckily she didn't have to figure it out. A waitress chose that exact moment to come by and deliver a drink to each of them.

"*Ooh*, margaritas!" Liz cooed. "My favorite."

"From the gentleman in the corner," the waitress said, and as Liz turned to look, she dropped a small cocktail napkin with a handwritten note into Scarlett's lap with a conspiratorial glance.

"It's just like in the movies!" Liz continued to gush. "We've only just got here, and already we have a handsome admirer buying us drinks."

Scarlett searched the restaurant for the so-called gentleman in the corner and found him just seconds before Liz.

Henry Mitchell, III smiled from across the room and gave a tiny wave to acknowledge them.

"*Eew*," Liz said, making a fake gagging sound and pointing her finger down her throat. "He probably poisoned them."

"C'mon, don't be like that! I bet he's just congratulating us on a good race."

"Good for him, I bet. I wouldn't be surprised if he's the one who messed up your cart thingy."

Scarlett knew she had to play this carefully, but she still couldn't let Liz get away with such a terrible accusation when she knew nothing about the real Henry. She pointed out, "Shane already said it was his fault, so just calm down and drink your margarita."

"He's lucky I happen to love strawberry 'ritas." Liz sighed and took a long, slow drink from her glass. "You know, you're making a lot of excuses for him tonight. You don't still have feel—"

"No, of course not! Give it a break!"

Liz shrugged and slid out from the booth. "Whatever you say, Scar-Scar. I need to run to the bathroom. Hold our table? Looks like some of these vultures are just waiting for us to fly the coop."

"I'll order some loaded potato skins for us to enjoy once you get back from the 1950's... Oops, I mean the 'bathroom.'" Scarlett made air quotes, and Liz play-hit her with her purse before snaking her way through the crowd in search of the restroom.

The moment Liz disappeared behind the bathroom door, Scarlett smoothed the napkin out on the table. *Text me,* it said, and then gave a local number scrawled in a quick hand.

She glanced toward Henry who still stood by himself in

the corner. When he caught her eye, he lifted a finger to his lips and mouthed, "*Shh*."

She punched the number into her phone and named the new contact Lauren, just in case Liz happened to oversee. Then she sent her first message to Henry: *Thank you for the drinks.*

His reply came quickly. *You're welcome. You look great, by the way.*

She flushed at the compliment. Had Henry seen her walk in? Had he seen all the extra skin on display? She felt equal parts embarrassed and delighted by his response.

Her phone buzzed again.

I know your friend will flip if I come talk to you. So can we text?

Okay.

"I'm back!" Liz announced, sliding into the booth across from Scarlett. "What'd I miss?"

Scarlett slipped the phone into her lap and smiled up innocently at Liz. "Not much. The waitress hasn't been back yet."

"Doesn't she know I can't hold my liquor without some food to sop it up?" She laughed and licked some salt from the rim of her glass.

Scarlett took a small sip, too. "No, but I'll make sure to tell her when she comes back."

Her phone buzzed again, and she smiled when she

glanced at the new text from Henry. *You were like a super-star out there today. You would have won if your sled hadn't fallen apart.*

Thanks, she typed, as Liz went on about this uptight woman her father had recently started dating.

It was nice to see you again, she added to her conversation with Henry.

I wish I could talk to you again. Not like this, but for real. I can't stop thinking about you. The dance. The sled ride. The way your body felt tucked into mine.

The temperature in the room rose a million degrees, and Scarlett knew she'd turned firetruck red upon reading that last comment.

It didn't escape Liz's notice either. "Who are you texting with?" she asked, trying to get a glimpse of the small phone screen clutched to Scarlett's chest.

"Just an old work friend," she answered, because that was kind of true.

Liz smiled sadly. "Do you miss it? The library?"

"Sort of, but I've been so busy that I haven't had much time. As you already know."

"Oh, yeah, totally, but we should still stop in tomorrow before you leave back for Puffin Ridge. Want to?" she said after taking another huge gulp of her drink, which was almost halfway finished now.

"Yeah," Scarlett said as she tried to think of what she

could write back. Finally, she settled on *I think about those times, too.*

When this is all over and the media has moved on, let me take you out on a proper date.

How do I even know you'll still want to after all that time?

I'll always want you, Scarlett. Nothing is going to change that.

"What's your friend saying?" Liz asked, and Scarlett realized how rude she was being. This night was supposed to be about them, not some secret text conversation. She wished she could confide in her about her secret flirtations, but no. Liz had made her feelings on Henry Mitchell, III abundantly clear when her father had agreed to start training him—and, boy, had she given Scarlett an earful then.

"She says she misses me," Scarlett answered, only massaging the truth slightly.

"Well, I miss you, too. Put the phone down and be with me. Tell me what it felt like when the wheel snapped out from under you. Were you scared?"

With a tinge of regret, Scarlett locked her phone and put it into her purse, then she told Liz all about the rush of exhilaration she'd had as she rode the three-wheeled chariot toward the finish line.

Other than the few times she'd spent with Henry, it was the most exciting sixty seconds of her life.

CHAPTER 30

THE NEXT MORNING, SCARLETT AWOKE WITH A POUNDING headache. Even though she'd only had one margarita, the alcohol's effect had made her giddy all night, and now she had a serious case of the morning-afters. Liz, on the other hand, had ordered a second and a third, and still seemed bright-eyed and bushy-tailed when she awoke that day.

"*Ugh*, remind me to never drink again," Scarlett moaned as she noshed on a banana.

"What are you talking about? Last night was so much fun!" Liz slurped at an oversized mug of coffee, despite being a morning person without any extra caffeine to help her along.

"Yeah, it was pretty fun," Scarlett admitted and thought back to her secret texts with Henry.

"Do you really have to go so soon?" Liz asked with a sad look on her face.

"Yeah, but I promise it won't take me so long to come back for a visit this time."

"And I'll hold you to it, Missy. Now get gone before I change my mind and decide to hold you prisoner in my basement. Or, as your people say, *hike!*"

"Wow, so many things wrong with that statement. I think that's my cue to go." Scarlett gave her friend a quick hug goodbye, then started on the road that would deliver her back to Puffin Ridge.

She hadn't driven far when she remembered her plan to check in at the library while she was in town. As silly as it was, a part of her even missed the stodgy Mrs. Caputo. Plus, she was looking forward to meeting the new girl she'd be supervising when she returned to the stacks next year.

Stopping at a coffee shack on her way over, she ordered a small latte. But when her headache pulsed again, she asked for a large instead. Maybe caffeine and a few quick chapters of an exciting new book in a familiar, old place would be just the cure she needed for her mini hangover. After all, she had a long drive ahead of her.

At the library, the front desk appeared to be empty despite the growing number of patrons milling about the entryway. One of the regulars who liked to come by a few times per week saw Scarlett and waved.

"Hey, JoAnn!" Scarlett rushed over to give this familiar face a huge, happy grin. "It's been a good few weeks since I've seen you. How have you been?"

"Oh, my life is always the same," the older woman said with a massive smile of her own. "I've started a new Cozy series and have wished you were here to talk about it with. That other woman just isn't as friendly, is she?"

Scarlett laughed. "Mrs. Caputo? Maybe not, but don't tell her I agreed with you!"

JoAnn bobbed her head as she talked. "I've seen you on the news a couple times. It looks like the sledding adventure is going well."

"Oh, yes! I'm having such a great time."

She dropped her voice to a lower register now. "I'll admit, I was startled when I'd heard you quit. I thought you loved your job at the library, but now I can see that the change has suited you well."

Okay, that was surprising. JoAnn always had her nose where ever there was news to be sniffed out. How could she have gotten things so wrong about Scarlett's sabbatical?

"Quit? Who told you I quit?" Scarlett shook her head and offered a placating smile, but JoAnn's scowl only deepened.

"That same terse old woman. Mrs. Caputo, did you say?"

"Oh, I'm sure you just misunderstood. No, I'm on an extended leave. I'll be back in April." She tried to keep her voice steady, but worry niggled at her. JoAnn loved reading mysteries for a reason. She loved chasing down a good story and figuring out the who, what, and why. Could she have really misunderstood so completely—or was it Scarlett who had misunderstood?

JoAnn's brow furrowed as she switched from her usual head bob to a slow shake. "No, you definitely quit," she said slowly, emphasizing each word. "At least that's what I was told."

"*Hmm.*" Scarlett couldn't hide her upset now. "JoAnn, it's been so nice seeing you, but now you've got me nervous."

JoAnn transitioned back to her favored nod and waved Scarlett off. "And I'm nervous for you, dear! Go find that Mrs. Caputo and find out what's going on."

Well, nobody had to tell Scarlett twice. She only hoped she'd be able to control her temper enough to get a straight answer.

CHAPTER 31

SCARLETT PUSHED THROUGH THE DOORS INTO THE BACK offices of the library. Normally, she'd respect the quiet space, but right now she wanted to scream like a banshee—whatever it took to make sure she was heard.

Why would Mrs. Caputo have told everyone she quit? It just didn't make any sense.

The librarian's door was firmly closed, but Scarlett stormed straight through without knocking. If the old woman had been spreading rumors—or worse—than she didn't deserve this polite precaution from Scarlett.

"Scarlett, what are you doing here?" Mrs. Caputo asked from her place behind the desk without a single trace of guilt on her withered face.

"What are you doing while I'm not here?" Scarlett demanded, noticing now a third person sat in the office with them. She seemed familiar, though Scarlett couldn't quite place her.

"Ms. Cole, have a seat," the woman said as she rose and offered up her own chair.

Scarlett recoiled from the woman as she reached her hand toward her in greeting. "Who are you, and how do you know me?"

Mrs. Caputo cleared her throat and stated, "This is Vanessa Price. She's head of the budgetary committee."

Vanessa Price, of course. That's where Scarlett had seen her overdone, fake mask of a face—all over the sides of buses and newspaper ads. She'd only been elected fairly recently, but was apparently already very concerned with the goings-on at the library.

Scarlett gave a tight nod toward the politician, then turned back to her former supervisor and demanded an answer to her original inquiry. "Why would JoAnn Marples say that I quit?"

Mrs. Caputo mumbled something incoherent and shifted her gaze toward Mrs. Price, who wasted no time in providing an answer of her own.

"Because, my dear, you did."

Oh, Scarlett was growing to hate this woman more by the second. Thankfully, she had voted for the other guy. "What? That's ridiculous! I never—"

"You never left your job without first obtaining the

proper clearance?" Vanessa Price lowered herself to the desk and took a seat on the polished mahogany as if this was just some quaint conversation over morning tea.

At least Scarlett was taller than the other two women now. That gave her a little more confidence as she shouted, "But she gave me clearance! It was her idea!" She jabbed an angry finger at Mrs. Caputo, who simply frowned and looked to Mrs. Price.

"*Now, now.* We both know that she doesn't have that kind of authority. After all, this is a government-funded entity."

"But I didn't quit! I'm coming back in April. After the—"

"After the race?" The politician gave a phony chuckle. "More than one full year after you last reported to work? Nobody gets year-long sabbaticals, dear. Not even me."

"Okay then," Scarlett said, finally taking a seat. "I guess I'm coming back now."

It was now that Mrs. Caputo found her voice again, only to say, "Actually, you've already been fired for failure to report to work. We tried sending a notice, but it seems we didn't have your correct forwarding address."

"This is insane! You could have just called me. My cell number's the same. And I never would have left, if I didn't think— if she hadn't—*Ugh!*"

Vanessa Price nodded as she listened and gave Scarlett a pitying look. "I understand that you're frustrated, but it's really for the best. We've had to scale the budget way back this year. Even poor Mrs. Caputo had to delay her retirement. We couldn't support the full staff's salaries anyway."

This was going from bad to worse in a hurry. Would Scarlett go to jail if she decked a politician in the face? Would it be worth it, anyway?

"What budget cuts are you talking about? The library is a pillar of the community. No one would dare steal money from it, especially not some newbie politician who needs to keep her ratings up if she wants to see another term."

"Yes, well..." Vanessa's expression turned cold. "My constituents are quite happy with the new tourism initiative, regardless of what you may think."

"Tourism? You are seriously putting tourism over education? Over knowledge?" This was a bad dream. It had to be. Who would come after the library? Who would let them?

Mrs. Price was quick with an answer. "Not just me, the full board. We've had quite the opportunity with this whole Billionaire Bucket List story. It's like a perfectly packaged gift that fell right into our laps. The whole country has their eyes on Anchorage now. We'd be fools not to grab onto that brass ring while it presented itself."

"Billionaire...?" Her words trailed off. She knew exactly who and what was meant.

"Yes, Henry Mitchell, III. You know him, don't you? After all, he's your competitor."

"I…"

Mrs. Caputo rose from her chair and motioned toward the still open door. "You're about done here, don't you think, Scarlett?"

Scarlett looked from her former supervisor to her local congresswoman. Both wore hideous jack-o-lantern smiles.

"Yes, I think Mrs. Caputo has a point here," Vanessa said, now also motioning toward the door. "After all, it was you who decided to leave a perfectly stable government job in order to chase dogs around in the snow."

Scarlett couldn't fight back the burning tears that formed in her eyes. She didn't even care about keeping up appearances anymore. This hurt—deeply. "How could you talk about it like that? You act like you want what's best for this city, and then you make fun of one of our greatest pastimes?"

Vanessa smirked and rolled her eyes. "Stop being so dramatic. I'm only teasing."

"You'll never get away with this. Too many people care about the library to see you cut it apart for profit, and if nobody else will fight this, I will," she vowed.

"Okay, Scooby Doo. Go drive off in your little Mystery Machine now and stop meddling. The elected officials have already decided what's best for this city, and it no longer has anything to do with you."

"We'll see about that," Scarlett said before slamming the door behind her.

CHAPTER 32

SCARLETT STOMPED OUT OF THE LIBRARY, HER BRAIN A frantic whir. It felt as if she was spinning off the chariot all over again, only this time, the pain proved much worse.

She jammed her keys at the ignition, missed, and had to try again. When she missed a second time, she collapsed onto the steering wheel and allowed herself to cry big, mournful tears.

Far more than her job had been lost that day.

She couldn't live with Lauren and Shane forever, even if they agreed to take her in long-term as she expected they might. Married couples needed their space, and as a grown woman herself, Scarlett needed some semblance of independence. If she couldn't find library work in Anchorage, she'd either need to leave the state or leave the industry—both of which terrified her.

And this could be just the first of many libraries under fire. Would budget cuts continue to threaten these beacons of knowledge until the last one crumbled? She hated the thought that the world Ray Bradbury painted in *Farenheit 451* might actually become a reality one day. If the government decided books weren't important, what would they try to dismiss next? And what about all the children who would miss out on a lifelong love affair with reading?

No, she would stay and fight this. She would be an advocate—not just for herself, but for libraries everywhere. This newfound resolve comforted her enough for now. At least she knew what she was up against. At least she knew she'd been fired.

She dabbed at her eyes with a long sleeve and fastened her seat belt, ready for the long drive back to Puffin Ridge. She'd be alone with her thoughts, and that was when her best ideas came.

As she reached for the gearshift, her phone buzzed in the cup holder, its sound magnified as the metal and glass vibrated against the plastic.

A text message.

From Henry.

Could he have known about this? Had he met secretly with Vanessa Price as he had done with Scarlett? Did he agree to be the face of her ridiculous tourism campaign? Did he know what he was helping to destroy?

She put the car back into park and unlocked her phone to see his message.

Thinking of you. Hope you're having a good day :)

Scarlett considered ignoring his message as she drove home, but knew it would eat at her if she did. So she decided to take this opportunity to fish for a bit of information instead. At least then some of her many questions would be answered.

I met Vanessa Price today, she typed and hit send.

Yeah? About time she included you in the campaign. Your pretty face will bring in lots of visitors.

She held her breath, hoping that her instincts were wrong, that Henry would have seen this plan for what it is, that he would have said no. *The campaign?*

You know, the Anchorage is Cool travel ads.

Scarlett groaned at the stupid name as well as the fact that Henry was obviously involved on the ground floor. *Oh, yes. And you think they're a good idea? The ads?*

Absolutely! Tourism is good for the economy. It makes sense they'd want to bring more to the city.

Scarlett's tears returned in earnest. Henry was so sure that he wasn't anything like his grandfather, yet here he was making decisions based on profit rather than heart. *But what about the budget cuts that had to be made to support the campaign's expense?*

Not a big deal. Once more money comes in from the

travelers, I'm sure there will be more than enough of the budget to go around.

And in the mean time?

She hated what he typed next. *Well, you can't have progress without sacrifice. Wouldn't you agree?*

The tears fell so fast they blurred the phone as she wrote, *No, I don't agree! I lost my job! The library is in danger of being expensed out of existence! And you know about it!*

Scarlett, let me call you.

The phone rang in her hand a few short moments later, but she rejected the call. She had her answers and didn't want to hear anything more until she could come up with a solution.

He tried calling again. This time, she let it ring out until the switch to voicemail.

Scarlett, please, Henry typed and called a third time.

She turned her phone off, cranked up the radio as loud as it would go with the hope that it would drown out her thoughts, and began the drive home to Puffin Ridge.

Everyone said Henry Mitchell, III was no good, but she'd thought she knew better. She thought she saw something more in him. Turned out he was just another no-good businessman.

And this whole "I'm really a good guy act?"

Either he was lying to her... or to himself.

CHAPTER 33

WHEN SCARLETT FINALLY REACHED THE CABIN IN PUFFIN Ridge, she crept straight to her room and shut herself inside, incapable of discussing the events of that day with her best friends even though she knew she would need to soon. She wanted to scream into her pillow or pretend it was Vanessa Price and give it a few good punches, but neither of those would help to solve the actual problems she faced.

The biggest of all these was that she could no longer trust herself. She'd been wrong about Mrs. Caputo's motives and—even more painfully—about Henry's heart. How could she have messed up so badly? One moment she thought she was on the verge of maybe, actually, *impossibly* placing in the Iditarod and finding love all in one go. The next, she found out it was all a lie.

Henry had probably only flirted with her to work some

kind of story angle because, sure enough, footage of them dancing at the Miners and Trappers Ball and then them exchanging a few quick words at the Hozier Track starting line were already being pasted together to tell a tale of love turned hate.

Local bookworm hooks a hottie!

From sweet nothings to angry barbs!

Lovers turned rivals in the dog-sledding world!

The headlines went on and on. Why did any of them care about her, especially when there was so little to tell? How could such sensational bullcrap flourish when actual books were left to languish at the hands of an under-sized staff?

What would be next?

Would they convert the children's section of her beloved library into a fast food playland? Would they undermine everything else the library did for the community and shut it down in favor of a more budget-conscious online eBook lending system?

And was it just the politicians who were to blame, or had the larger society changed when she wasn't paying close enough attention to notice? Did the world really need half a dozen articles about the non-news of Scarlett and Henry? Was *this* what people chose to read instead of literature?

The thought made her stomach churn and her heart roil.

Outside, a car pulled up to the cabin, and she peeked

through the window, wishing she'd have had just a little more time to sort out her thoughts before Shane and Lauren arrived back home.

But the person she saw approaching her window now wasn't Shane or Lauren. It was Henry.

And he saw her, too. His mismatched eyes caught hers, and he quickened his pace.

Scarlett slammed the blinds down, but he came to the window anyway and tapped gently on the glass. "I know you're there. Please talk to me."

Scarlett crossed her arms over her chest and fell back on her bed, unwilling to make a peep.

His voice came out strained and soft. Had he been crying, too?

"I didn't know you lost your job. I didn't even know you had a job other than handling. I didn't know the library was on the chopping block, and I didn't know it was so important to you."

At last she could hold her anger back no more. She had to speak up. "It doesn't matter that it's important to me," she thundered. "It's important, *period*. How could you not understand that?"

"Will you come out, or let me in?" he begged. His pleading only made her angrier.

"I have nothing more to say to you! I should've listened

to what everyone said about you. I shouldn't have let you trick me just to get a little extra news coverage."

"Is that really what you think of me?" His voice cracked, but she didn't care.

He tapped a slow sad tune on the window pane, then whispered through the glass, "I was trying to help do something good. I wanted to help people appreciate this great state and this sport which I'd started to love for myself, not just because of that dumb bucket list. I didn't know the fine details about the budgeting decisions. I'm just the face of the campaign, Scarlett. I thought I was helping to—"

She thrust the blinds up, stopping him midsentence. "You're wasting your breath. I won't change my mind, and Lauren and Shane won't be happy to see you here. You need to leave. Now."

His eyes glistened with tears. Oh, he could put on a good show, but she refused to be tricked again.

"But, Scarlett, please," he whispered. "I'll do anything. When I get the money from the estate, I'll fund the library myself. I'll have them hire you back. I'll—"

"No!" she shouted as she slammed the blinds down again and fell onto the bed in a heap of tears. "You think money is the solution to all of life's problems, but..."

She cried freely and he waited for her to deliver the final blow to their budding relationship. "Deny it all you want, but you're just like him, Henry. You're exactly like your granddad."

As enraged as she was, the words stung even her on their way out, but they had to be said. They had to be. She was nobody's fool, least of all some spoiled rich boy with a blackened heart.

Her visitor said nothing more, and a few minutes later, she heard his Mercedes reverse back out of the driveway. This time for good.

CHAPTER 34

Scarlett trained harder than ever before, throwing herself full force at the sport. After all, it was the only thing she had left now. As expected, Lauren and Shane had offered a full-time position with room and board, but she flatly refused. They didn't need a full-time handler, and she needed to solve her problems for herself.

In the months that followed, she worked hard to forge a grueling physical routine, to leave herself no time to dwell on anything but the upcoming race.

Early each morning, after feeding the "veterans," she would hook up the puppies and run them in a tight circle with an empty sled behind them as she led the dogs through their paces. In this way, she was able to act as the lead dog and get her blood pumping as well.

Then after a quick breakfast, she would hook up

Lauren's team and take them for a workout around the property, normally sticking to twenty miles or so. She didn't like running Lauren's team as much as her own, but figured she'd need as much practice as possible because she was cramming for the biggest test in her life.

And she planned to pass with flying colors. She'd already passed the qualifying races and knew she had a place in the main event that year. What happened next would depend on how hard she trained and how well she focused, so she did just that, leaving little time for anything—or anyone—else.

For lunch, she would stop into the house and give Lauren a report on how her team did for the morning run and quiz Shane on any questions she'd come up with while out on the trail. She'd given up on reading books for her answers after the debacle at the library and when she'd made the mistake of reading a guide from a musher that was very much of the same mindset as Henry's grandfather.

Whenever her thoughts turned to Henry, as they still inevitably did whenever she let her guard down, she would busy herself by working to further rehabilitate Fantine and the other rescue dogs. A few had adjusted well already and had already begun to crave running again, so three times a week she would hook them up and take them for short runs, too.

Before dinner, she would hook up "her" team. They were always excited to see her coming around with harnesses in hand. Fred would make sure to give her large, sloppy kisses when she got close enough to his little hut.

The days passed quickly this way. She woke up early and went to bed late, pushing her body to its limits and enjoying the newfound strength, both of muscles and of will. Shane and Lauren often exchanged pointed glances that suggested they spoke about her when she wasn't around, that they worried about her—but she ignored their concerns.

She pushed harder, harder, harder, driven by both love and hate as she prepared for the upcoming Iditarod. It wouldn't be long now. Even Fantine's puppies had already neared their adult weights now. The world was speeding forward with or without Scarlett, and she did everything in her power to keep up.

One day she noticed one of the puppies, Lenny, looking at her wistfully as Scarlett readied her team for their after-dinner run.

"Hey there, little guy," she cooed to the giant puppy. At just about five months old, he was already the same size as a few of the leaner dogs. She'd definitely named him right. "You want to go running with everyone else?"

He yowled in response—a special husky noise that showed just how excited he was. He'd done well in the mornings, so what could it hurt to give him a shot with the big dogs? Without giving any further thought to the matter, she harnessed him up and hooked him onto the sled. His eyes were wild with excitement, and for the first time, Scarlett noticed that like his mother, he had heterochromia. Though his discoloration wasn't as pronounced, one blue eye was clearly darker than the other. Had they changed since birth, or had she just never looked at him closely enough before? It seemed odd, given all the time she spent in the company of the dogs and especially the puppies.

But she pushed the worry from her mind, lest her thoughts return to another person she knew with mismatched eyes—Henry. Instead of having Lenny run next to another dog, she left Lenny on his own. Normally, dogs would run in pairs, but Scarlett wanted to make sure he was going to be okay hooked to the big sled before she tried to pair him up. Then, like she'd done every day, she hollered to the dogs and away they went.

She'd expected Lenny to be a bit nervous with the bigger sled or the longer track, but he took to the new system like a duck to the water. Or rather, a sled dog to the snow. They took a shorter run, but by the end of it, she knew that Lenny had been born to race.

She told Lauren and Shane as much that night over dinner.

"You got one of the pups to go out with your team today?" Shane asked. "I'm impressed."

"Which one?" Lauren asked, bringing over another delicious plate of vittles.

"Lenny," Scarlett responded through forkfuls.

Shane laughed. "Well, he hardly counts a puppy. He's practically the size of half the dogs out there."

"You think you've got a new favorite?" Lauren asked. "Fred'll be heart-broken, but by the time the Iditarod comes around, Lenny will probably be bigger than him."

"Sometimes hearts break," Scarlett answered with a shrug.

Shane and Lauren exchanged that well-practiced look, the one they always made when Scarlett's behavior had started to concern them.

Lauren cleared her throat. "*Umm*, so we were thinking about heading into Anchorage next weekend. Meeting up with a few other mushers, just a casual get-together. We were wondering if—"

Scarlett held up her hand. "No, I'm just going to hang out here and see if I can find out who Lenny likes to run beside. If he's going to be as big as you think, it might be good to have him with me on the way to Nome."

Shane looked like he was about to say more, but Lauren brushed his arm and gave him that look again. He slowly rose with the help of his cane and an excuse about a TV program he wanted to watch, then left the women on their own.

"Okay, spill," Lauren said. "What's gotten into you?"

"You know what's gotten into me. I lost my job and all I have left is this race. I have to do my best."

"Are you sure? Because it seems like a whole lot more than that. You're not yourself lately, Scar."

"I'm exactly who I've always been. Just my competitive side has come out now."

"No, Scarlett. This isn't who you are, and frankly, sometimes you scare me these days. You know you can talk to me about anything, right?"

Scarlett sighed. "I know."

"What's wrong?"

"Everything," Scarlett said on a sob. "Everything's wrong, and I'm doing my best to make it right again, but what if my best isn't enough?"

"Oh, Scar. We'll figure it out together. I promise, Shane and I are here for you."

She almost told Lauren everything in that moment. Almost told her of her attraction to Henry, their heated sled ride and secret texts, the inevitable betrayal that followed.

Almost.

But instead, she took another bite of dinner and swallowed her feelings down—down so deep she hoped they would drown.

CHAPTER 35

SCARLETT USED HER MOMENTARY FAME TO CREATE something she hoped would be more permanent. Now, instead of avoiding the cameras, she called them over and gave them the carefully constructed soundbites they craved.

Now they knew her name and cited it often in their sports sections.

"Scarlett, is it true that you've vowed to beat Henry Mitchell, III, no matter what it takes?" they asked.

And, oh, did she answer!

She said things like, "The first Henry Mitchell was an evil man who did terrible things to the sport and our great state. The third is no better. I'm racing to prove that any man—or woman—has what it takes, that you don't have to be born with a silver spoon in your mouth to take a bite out of life. Strength of will is power, but so is strength of knowledge. That's why it's so important we save our libraries and stop politicians like Vanessa Price who want to tear them down in order to pad her retirement. I hope you'll join me in writing to Congress to express your disappointment. Thank you."

And the reporters ate it right up. An investigation was launched into Vanessa Price's budgetary practices, but no wrongdoing had been uncovered—at least not yet. Scarlett was certain the woman hid far more than anyone knew.

In fact, it seemed that Mrs. Price actually loved all the press attention. She even began to turn up at races, standing proudly at Henry's side. And she always made sure the race officials stationed Scarlett and Henry right beside each other at the starting line to play into the drama. Even Ben Benjamin gave in to these requests before too long.

"It's good for the sport, sweet pea," he said with a shrug when Liz confronted him about it.

"She probably has her hooks in him, too," Scarlett spat when her friend recounted the conversation.

"I don't know what's going on," Liz answered, "but I definitely don't like it. It's as if Dad has forgotten what that woman did to you. Either that or he's forgiven her, and I honestly don't know which is worse... She came over for dinner the other night," Liz revealed after a painful pause.

What?

Guilt grabbed hold of Scarlett's conscience, and this time

it refused to let go. If she hadn't introduced Henry to Ben, then Ben wouldn't have been corrupted. And what did this mean for poor Liz? Scarlett had definitely been a very poor friend to her these past few months, and she needed to fix that now.

"Are they dating?" she asked, unable to conceal the disgust in her voice.

Liz moaned. "I think so. Oh, Scar, what am I going to do?"

"You're going to move out of there until your dad comes to his senses. Once I win this race, we'll get an apartment all our own and we'll start over. If you need a place sooner, let me know. Otherwise, I'm going to offer my subletter the chance to take over my lease fully. If you need the apartment, say the word and it's yours."

Liz hugged her tightly and let out a squeal. "My Scar-Scar is back at last!"

Scarlett wondered what it meant that one of her friends thought she had changed completely while the other claimed she was finally being herself again.

Moreover, which Scarlett was the real one, and which was the imposter?

CHAPTER 36

With time, Scarlett actually began to enjoy her interactions with the press. She'd always known words had power, but seeing their might firsthand brought a whole new appreciation to this once disgraced librarian. She started working out what she'd say in advance, arranging and rearranging her words until they were perfect.

The absence of words had power, too.

Henry had texted a few more times after his visit to the cabin that fateful day, but Scarlett had refused to answer and eventually blocked his number. At first, he'd tried to speak kindly to her at race events, but she only ever responded with sharp replies, the kind that put the reporters into a frenzy, the kind they loved to write about while covering the so-called star-crossed rivals.

Still, even with this new rush, her heart hurt whenever

she looked at Henry. She tried to hide it, but some of the savvier reporters had picked up on that longing.

"I could never fall for a man who stands for everything I hate in this world," she'd said when asked about it. "He's fire, and I'm ice. Guess which of those wins the Iditarod?"

And Henry served these volleys right back her way in his interviews. "Scarlett Cole," he was often quoted as saying, "should keep her nose in books and out of this sport. She doesn't have the training. She doesn't have the ability. And she doesn't *have the heart*. Ms. Cole seems to think that anyone can stand on the back of a sled and let the dogs pull them to victory, but are we forgetting that she couldn't even manage that at the Tozier event? Mark my words, she can't win. She won't even place."

They spent time together in this new way. At least she imagined they did— each reading over what the other had said and preparing the perfect counter-strike, picturing the look on the rival's face when finally word got out.

"Why do you hate him so much?" Lauren had asked one day.

"You hate him, too," Scarlett had answered quickly, defensively.

Lauren shook her head gently. "But it's not the same."

"He stands for everything I hate. He's fire, and I'm ice," Scarlett supplied from rote.

"Yeah, I know what you tell the press, but I'm asking as your friend."

"There's a fine line between love and hate," Scarlett said and then sighed. "Sometimes I forget which side I've placed him on."

When Lauren pressed for more, Scarlett just shrugged and said, "I've made mistakes, but I'm learning from every single one of them. Thinking there was any humanity inside Henry Mitchell, III's heart was perhaps the biggest mistake of all."

And with that, their rivalry grew and her gentler memories of their time spent together were mostly replaced with these heated exchanged.

Mostly.

But not all.

CHAPTER 37

FINALLY, THE BIG DAY ARRIVED. AT LONG LAST, THE Iditarod was here.

Scarlett looked out across the sea of faces lined up on the Anchorage streets. Shane and Rosie had opted not to ride in the basket for the ceremonial start this year. Instead, they stood amongst the spectators waving signs they'd hand-painted and dusted with glitter, alternating between cheering for Lauren and cheering for Scarlett.

After biting the thumb of her glove and pulling it off, she used her bare fingers to double-check all the connections on both dogs and sled. She'd been pleasantly surprised when Shane had shown her the team in full regalia. Fred, Lenny, and the rest of the boys were decked out in green racing bibs with purple booties on their feet. Wendy and the other girls were dressed in the reverse—purple bibs with green booties.

Unlike a lot of the other teams, her team stood still, tensed against the anchor of the snow hook. They didn't jump or bark or play, almost as if they sensed how serious a moment this was for Scarlett. She adjusted the front end of her sled and made sure to give Fred a pat on the back.

"You ready for this, boy?"

Fred stamped in response and bit at the purple bootie on one of his front feet.

They'd be starting soon, but she still hadn't given an interview.

She glanced toward Ben Benjamin, who stood busy with his clipboard as usual during these events. Vanessa Price appeared at his side, resting her head on his shoulder for a brief moment. But it was enough to send a clear message, especially when the vile woman looked straight at Scarlett and smiled. The gesture just wasn't natural for her, despite how often she had to put it to use for political purposes.

That smile was either a taunt or a warning, but it didn't matter which to Scarlett. Either way, she would beat Henry, beat Vanessa—she'd even beat the man who had once been like a father to her if he insisted on aligning himself with the two of them. She would show them all. She would win at whatever sick game they were playing, even though she had yet to understand the rules.

She swallowed the angry lump of unformed words in her throat and stalked toward the press to give them a piece of her mind and offer one last quote for their papers, but Shane stopped her with a firm hand on her shoulder.

"Don't," he said.

"I'm just going to—"

"I know what you're going to, and I'm telling you that you shouldn't."

"Shane, listen—"

"No, you've been doing a lot of talking lately. Too much talking. I need you to listen."

She let out an irritated huff but let Shane continue.

"You confided in me that day on the chariot, and I've kept my promise to you. Lauren doesn't know anything more than the little you've told her. But I need you to understand something about anger. If you let it, it will take over everything. It will strangle your life like vines, kill everything. I was so lost. I thought if I gave everything to the dogs, then I wouldn't hurt anymore. Just like you're doing now. But that doesn't work."

She was growing impatient with him. Why couldn't he have given this speech earlier if it was so important? "Okay, so what's your point?"

"My point is you can't go out there like this, Scarlett. You're too angry, and that anger's a distraction. Look at me." He frowned and held up his cane emphatically. "I was distracted on a simple practice run, and now I'm out of the race forever. I could have lost so much more that day."

"But it all turned out all right for you. You have Lauren now. You're happy."

"Yes," Shane said, placing a hand on each of her shoulders and letting his cane fall to the ground at his side. "But you're not. You saw the good in Henry once. Try to see it again. You don't have to forgive him, but you need to let it go for your own good."

"Shane, I appreciate what you're trying to do here, but I know how to take care of myself and the dogs out there. I'll be fine." She stooped to pick up his cane and return it to him. "Give Rosie a hug for me, and tell her I'll see her in a few days. But first, I've got a race to win."

CHAPTER 38

THE WIND HAD ALREADY BEGUN TO BITE AT SCARLETT'S cheeks. Normally she'd have stopped a training run by now, tied the dogs back up, given everyone some rest. But this was the big one. Nobody took potty breaks during the great race, and Scarlett had more of a reason to win than any of them. So what if she was a rookie? So what if she'd had to finish her first official race on foot? The only thing that mattered now was pushing herself and her dogs to their limits—and then going past even that.

As the sled continued its Northern trek, the air grew colder and colder, and Scarlett had to flex her toes inside her boots to make sure they retained feeling. She'd trained hard for this, but nothing had quite prepared for the actual longevity of the Iditarod. It could be two full weeks for her on the back of that sled.

They said there was a certain inevitability that one day, the great race would have to come to end. Scarlett knew that when it did, Alaska would lose a part of its soul. And maybe so would she.

Thank goodness for the checkpoints scattered along the path to Nome. Without them, Scarlett doubted she would even remember to eat or sleep. So badly she wanted to finish —and finish well. And it was that pressing desire for victory that fueled her forward. When she'd first started going out with Lauren on the sled, she'd marveled at the pretty snow, how the wind made it feel like she was flying. Now she hardly noticed those things.

She was all business now, and luckily her friend understood that and helped to offer little bits of advice whenever they ran into each other at a check-in.

"Don't work too hard to be in the lead right now," Lauren had confided in her. "Make someone else break the trail for you. And don't let all the stares bug you. They might be surprised that a rookie is doing this good, but I'm not."

At that thought, Scarlett glanced around the tiny outpost, surprised to see that there were very few others at the checkpoint with them. She'd been so focused on her own team that she hadn't noticed that she was consistently coming into the checkpoints just a couple hours behind the head of the pack.

"Just remember," Lauren had said that first night, "we've

got two mandatory rests to make. One's eight hours and one's twenty-four. You can take the big one anywhere, but the first eight-hour needs to be taken along Yukon. After that, we've got another eight hours in White Mountain."

Scarlett nodded, flexing her hands to circulate the blood.

"Scar," Lauren warned when she saw how preoccupied her friend's mind was with other things. "This is important. Don't feel like you have to push to leave the checkpoints as soon as you get there. The dogs come first. Take care of them, take care of you, and when you're ready, get back on the trail. I know you've said you're going to do this, but there's no shame in scratching."

No shame in scratching? She doubted Henry would drop out of the race. And neither would she.

Catching the concerned expression on Scarlett's face, Lauren circled back, "No, I don't suspect that you'll need to with as good as you're doing. I just know that things can happen out on the trail, and, well...if you need to scratch for the safety of your dogs or your health, do it."

Scarlett agreed to stay safe, but secretly she knew she would push if she needed to. She would never endanger her dogs, and luckily, she knew they were ready for this.

Back out on the trail, Scarlett focused on the path in front of her as she ventured through a part of the state that most people would never see. The so-called Last Frontier was every bit as dangerous and beautiful as Jack London had described it in his books. Scarlett silently kicked herself now for not having named one of the puppies after a character from one of his works.

As she pulled into the checkpoint at Ruby, Scarlett noticed an unsteadiness in Fred's gait. She quickly checked in with the race official and returned to examine her favorite dog. He was agitated now, stamping red foot prints in the snow. He'd somehow managed to remove one of his purple booties and flung it to the side.

No, no, no, she thought. *I need Fred. He's my wheel dog. He's my best.*

"It's okay, boy," she soothed the dog before running off to find an assigned vet.

The vet talked calmly as she examined Fred, then told Scarlett, "Looks like he's gotten ice in his pads, and it's caused a cut. You can rest him here. A lot of mushers choose this checkpoint as their eight-hour layover. If he's doing better, you can bandage the foot and reboot him and see if he'll run, but chances are you'll have to drop him here."

Scarlett waited the requisite eight hours, but sleep was hard to come by. She hoped her team was doing better outside. So many worries swirled together in her mind like a blizzard. Would Fred be able to continue on? Would she be able to compete without him? And what about Henry? She still didn't know whether he was ahead of her or behind. Unlike Lauren, she hadn't seen him since the beginning.

When at last the wait was up, she rushed to find the vet to get a prognosis on Fred, but had to wait while the woman finished an exam for another dog.

Scarlett tried to be strong for Fred and the other dogs, but inside, she was breaking apart like Alaska in the springtime. "Fred, buddy. I'm sorry. I'm so, so sorry. You tried to tell me back in Anchorage, didn't you?" she said, thinking back to the way he had stamped his foot impatiently at the starting lineup. "I'm sorry I didn't understand you then."

The vet came over to them then and bent down to check on Fred's paw. "Seems we have a bit of good news this morning. Fred looks like he's already on the mend. It was a small cut, and it's doing much better. You've got about fifty miles to Galena from here. Take him out, and if he starts showing signs that he's not going to be able to race, put him in the basket and drop him in Galena. The choice is yours." She gave Fred a loving stroke between the ears. "And his. Good luck out there. Godspeed."

Scarlett thanked her for the help, and once the vet left to check on the other teams, asked, "What do you say, Fred? Want to go on? Or are you done?"

Fred shook himself off and yipped happily at her.

"Atta boy," she said, giving him a nice scratch between the ears. "We're not out of this yet!"

CHAPTER 39

As Scarlett waited for her clearance to continue, another sled pulled up to the checkpoint.

"Well, well, Billionaire Bucket List," she greeted Henry with an energetic laugh, feeling well-rested from the night before. "Looks like money really can't buy everything."

"We're biding our time, reserving energy," Henry said as he went down the line, checking each of his dogs. "We're only just getting started. What was that you liked to call me? Fire to your ice? Well, prepare to eat smoke."

"We'll see about that," Scarlett said as the checkpoint motioned for her to continue. "Hike!" she shouted to the dogs and they were off.

Biding his time, sure. A part of her wondered what would happen to Henry and his family when he lost the race and thus his grandfather's estate, but that wasn't her problem. *He could have kept things civil. He's the one who made them personal,* she reminded herself.

More snow had fallen in the last eight hours, so the trail was harder to make out now. Still, they made it to Galena only a bit slower than average. And best of all, Fred showed no signs of being done with the race.

A miracle! It had to be. God was on her side.

Once the dogs were taken care of at the Galena checkpoint, Scarlett hurried back out to the trail. Now she knew Henry trailed her closely and could easily catch up to her during one of her layovers. She needed a big lead on him by then.

She stepped back onto the rack and popped a new warming pack into each mitten. "What do you say, pups? Shall we score a victory for the bookworms?"

Fred howled in response, bringing a smile to her face as she called, "Hike!"

After the required twenty-four-hour layover in Huslia, Scarlett had officially finished half the Iditarod. As the race wore on, a strange mix of muscle memory and fatigue kicked in. Checkpoints came and went as she wound her way to Nome. While her body knew just what to do, her energy was lagging. It became harder and harder to focus her thoughts on the movements of the sled, and she found her mind drifting.

To Mrs. Caputo. To Vanessa Price. To Henry.

Shane had told her to put her anger aside, but she preferred to harness it. Use it as a driving force forward as she flew through the Alaskan wilderness toward a dream that was so close to being realized at last.

The miles passed. The warmers lost their heat, and the cold set in again.

A yelp of pain sent shivers down her spine.

No, no, no! She was terrified to look, but she knew she owed it to the dogs to make sure they were well taken care of. Sure enough, Fred's limp had returned as he struggled to put minimal weight on his injured paw.

Muttering a few choice words under her breath, Scarlett commanded the sled to a stop and took Fred off the line.

"I'm sorry, buddy. You tried your best, and I'm proud of you." She wrapped Fred in a special bag that would keep him secure in the sled's basket.

The contraption left only Fred's head exposed, and she gave him a few extra pets to ease the worry in his sky blue eyes. "It's okay, my little husky burrito. You did your best, and you *almost* made it to the end. But your race is over for now. I'm going to strap you in so you can't try to pull the sled anyway, because I can tell if I left it to you, you'd run yourself into the ground."

Just like me, she thought with a grimace.

As they started to run again, Fred whined and struggled, wanting so desperately to be back on his feet. Her heart went out to him. She understood that dog, related to him, and she'd hate to be in his position now.

"There's no shame in scratching," Lauren had said. But no, she was down a dog. The rest of them would work harder to overcome the loss. They had to do this now more than ever. For Fred.

"Usually, I tell this story to Fantine, but today I'm going to tell it to you," she told the dog before launching into the epic story of Jean Valjean and Javert. To his credit, Fred looked up at her from his vantage point on the sled and appeared to listen intently.

Scarlett laughed. She would miss him once she dropped him off at the next checkpoint, and now she missed Fantine and the others who had been left back at the cabin, too. "Don't look at me, Fred, look at the view," she scolded. "It's got to be better than looking at Lenny's butt all day."

As she tried to recall the story of *Les Miserables* well enough to share it with her furry friend, she thought about everything the story had set out to say about the human condition. Sometimes right is wrong, and wrong is right. Sometimes we can't escape who we are, but sometimes we can band together and win the day. Like her and the dogs now. Was she Javert in this analogy… or Jean Valjean? Always in the habit of choosing the character she most identified with in any book, movie, or play, Scarlett was at a loss now. A part of her identified with each of the characters, yet another part couldn't understand either.

Maybe she wasn't a character in a book after all.

Maybe she was just Scarlett Cole, heroine of her own life.

Not many people would ever read it, but maybe that didn't matter just so long as those who got the chance appreciated having done so.

CHAPTER 40

When at least Scarlett's team pulled into White Mountain a full hour later than she had hoped, she was pleased to see Lauren waiting outside.

"I had a feeling you might be coming in just behind me." Her friend greeted her with a hug, which was especially welcome because of the extra warmth it provided. "How are you holding up? How is your team doing? How are *you* doing?"

Scarlett broke down in her friend's arms. She was too tired now. She had been strong for too long. A good cry could fix everything if she let it. Everything except the fact that her best dog was no longer at her side. "It's F-f-f-Fred!" she wailed.

And Lauren patted Scarlett on the back and helped get

her team situated next to her own. The two groups of dogs were excited to be reunited, even if it was just for a short while.

"I'm on hour three of my required eight hour layover here," Lauren said once the dogs were well situated. "You've got a full eight hours to go before you can race on to Nome. We'll give Fred some extra love before I call Shane to arrange Fred's return home. Okay?"

Scarlett agreed, unhappy about the need to stop and rest, but also relieved to be spending it with her best friend in the whole world.

"I cried my first time, too," Lauren said with a comforting grin. "You know last year? I think these big, burly lumberjack types do, too. They just hide it a little better."

Tears still mottled Scarlett's cheeks when Henry pulled into the checkpoint later that evening.

"Ignore him. Don't pay him any mind," Lauren warned. "That's what he wants—to psych you out, but he doesn't realize what a smart cookie my bestie is."

Lauren's team left several hours before Scarlett was allowed to resume her race. Once her friend had checked out, she spent the rest of her break next to Fred on his mound of straw. She told herself it was to ease his upset about missing the next part of the race, but truthfully, she just couldn't stand the thought of Henry glaring at her.

Because, yes, even now, his eyes followed her movements around the track points, the trails, wherever the two came into contact. It made her feel hot, like melting ice—and she just didn't need that now. She'd have to work even harder to compensate for Fred's loss.

There could be no distractions, especially since the weather was deteriorating fast. By the time Scarlett and the remaining dogs resumed their trek, snow and sleet were coming down in dangerous sheets. So far, she'd been fairly lucky to have had such a temperate race. But now, Mother Nature seemed to want to make up for the miles of fair weather with this sudden onslaught.

The Iditarod was known for putting both dog and musher through their paces, taking them to the brink—and now it seemed that the race itself wanted to test her. Well, she'd been studying for this test her whole life, and like the ancient motto of the postman, she was determined that neither snow, sleet nor dark of night would stop her from finishing right.

The trail conditions weren't ideal, but even still, several options stretched out before her. Left was the hillier trail, full of narrow paths into the sea. To her right, several rivers flowed out to the ocean. This time of year they would likely be frozen, but she didn't want to chance it. She opted to take a higher path to circumvent the rivers and any possibility of an ice break.

It would be a tight fit, but she'd rather be smushed than drowned. Few mushers were ahead of her right now, which meant it was up to her to find her way. Shane's voice briefly echoed in the back of her mind, but she pushed it aside and headed into the foot hills.

With a few false starts, she found her path and the dogs eagerly took to it. As the team raced on through the winds and sleet, Scarlett tapped on her headlamp to make sure she could see. Her line of sight didn't extend past Lenny running beside Wendy in Fred's place.

She needed to rely on the lead dogs now. They could see where she couldn't, and hopefully the bond they'd formed during training would be enough for them to anticipate her choices. That was what she needed most now—faith.

And so she prayed for a safe passage, quieting her mind to everything but the words whispered to God above. She'd chosen this, or He'd chosen it for her. Either way, they would get through this together.

Scarlett squeezed her eyes tight for the briefest of moments, trying to visualize the finish line, her and her team crossing it safely and to victory.

The sled jolted at a sharp turn, startling her eyes back open, although Scarlett still couldn't see more than a couple arms lengths. She leaned the other way to balance the sled, keep it on track. Had Fred been there, it would have worked.

But they'd left Fred back in White Mountain, and Lenny just didn't have the experience to overcome such a large blip.

The young husky balked, and that slight moment of hesitation was all it took to send the sled hurtling over the edge of the slope, a sinking anchor dragging Scarlett and the dogs down into the ice.

CHAPTER 41

Cold water splashed across Scarlett's chest as she broke through the ice. Howls rose into the night air, and she didn't know whether they were the dogs' or her own. Everything hurt and burned from the bitter cold. Her chest grew heavy and impossibly hard to lift with each staggered breath.

She was drowning, dying. And for the briefest of moments, the cold feeling abated. It felt warmer somehow, being surrounded by the water's embrace. She closed her eyes and wondered if it would really be the worst thing, dying doing what she loved...

And then a frantic pair of paws scratched at her chest.

Lenny!

She'd vowed to protect him as a puppy, and he needed her now. They all did.

With a tremendous effort, she kicked and propelled

herself toward the shore. Holding on to Lenny and the sled, she struggled to keep feeling in her extremities. Each movement took an enormous amount of strength to execute as her muscles and the blood within her veins both began to freeze. But she'd trained long and hard for this. She was stronger now and braver, too.

Back on land, movements were just as difficult as they'd been in the water. She now had to support her own body weight as well as that of the heavy clothes that had already turned to robes of ice.

"Don't... give... up," she grunted, unsure whether she was talking to herself or to Lenny, who still thrashed about in the water rather than coming up to the land at her side.

Panic rising to a fever pitch, she realized that the dogs were literally tied to an anchor. The sled had landed close to the shore and the dogs were still harnessed to it. Lenny was stuck to the others. She needed to get them all out together.

But as each husky, eskimo dog, malamute, and mutt struggled in the water, the line became more and more tangled. These dogs were used to working in a team, though they'd never faced a challenge like this before. Their survival instincts had kicked in, and that instinct shouted, "Every dog for himself!"

"Len-ny!' Scarlett cried, hacking out partially frozen breaths on either side of the word. "I need you to be strong for the others. Come to me!"

She fell to the frozen ground, ignoring the pain that shot through her knees when she did. All that mattered now was saving these dogs. They'd put their trust in her, and she couldn't let them down when it mattered most.

At the edge of the river, she took hold of the sled in both hands and began to drag it backward. She expected another jolt to her system, but it didn't come. Did this mean she'd already begun to lose feeling, her systems already on the path to shutting down for the big sleep? The final sleep?

She could still save the dogs.

Working with Lenny and Wendy, she continued to slowly pull the sled backward. Scarlett used the snow hook to help drag herself farther from the river. It became easier as more dogs reached the frozen ground and aided in the rescue effort. They were trained to pull, and they, too, knew the danger of this situation. They trusted Scarlett completely and did her bidding even as broken and frightened as they were.

Maybe hours, maybe only seconds had passed since their fall. To Scarlett, it felt as if time now stood still, a chasm with no past, no future, only now.

"*Hike! Hike! Hike!*" Scarlett chanted as loud as her broken voice would allow.

The dogs struggled forth, pulling away from the icy riverbank. Scarlett grabbed the basket and held on as she was pulled away with them.

At last, the full team was safely on land and away from the water. They'd done it. They'd managed to survive this first obstacle, but what came next? None of them had the strength to go any farther. They'd fallen off the trail, and with the snow coming down, there wouldn't be a trail anymore, which meant no one would know to look for them out here.

Scarlett knew then that she was going to die, but she could still save the dogs. Pulling off her soaked mittens, she worked her icy fingers at each of the harnesses. She struggled to free the dogs from the line, to give them the chance.

"Hike!" she cried weakly before at last collapsing into a bed of snow.

A warm tongue brought her back to herself.

The dogs. They still need me.

Scarlett fought through the pain to pull the dogs around to circle the wagons. In the middle, she pulled out her camp stove and the last couple bottles of Heet. Pouring out as much of the fuel as possible, she lit a small fire. Thankfully, most of her supplies were in dry bags. How Lauren knew she might need those, she could only guess.

Scarlett went through her checkpoint rituals, letting her body take over, her mind already impossibly trapped by the ice. The dogs got bits of meat from her pack and she worked on getting them all dried off. They dried quicker than she did, but the dogs came first. Always.

Once she was certain the dogs were okay, she flopped down next to the sled and peeled off the heaviest of her soaked layers. The cold wind stung but felt warmer than the water-logged parka.

The thick body of Lenny dropped onto her with a thud. She couldn't even feel the impact of the nearly eighty-pound dog against her chest. The fire continued to burn low, but the rest of the dogs crowded around her, warming her and licking her and taking care of her like she'd done for them.

She must've fallen asleep in the warm embrace of the sled team because when her eyes opened next, the fire had dulled to embers, and the colorful wonder of the Aurora Borealis stretched into the stars. Was this God's way of telling her she would be okay, or was she instead being welcomed through Heaven's gates?

As long as she was alive—however long that might be— she would fight. Although sharp pain stung at her feet, she needed to force herself up and stoke the fire to a blaze once more.

Sleep threatened to overtake her, but she needed to find the energy to keep going. Somewhere. Somehow. If they stayed here, they would all die. Even unhooked, the dogs would stay at her side until the last of them succumbed to winter's cold embrace.

It wouldn't be much longer now...

CHAPTER 42

Scarlett didn't remember closing her eyes to sleep, but when she opened them again, a blinding white light forced them shut once again. Her retinas stung, and her arms and legs felt like dead weights tying her to the earth.

She'd thought that the pain ceased in death, that she'd be weightless and free enough to stand on a cloud. The dogs barked and whimpered, some of them rising to their feet. She felt the movement all around her but couldn't see. It was either pitch black or blinding white, and neither gave her sight.

Floating now. Up toward Heaven, rising like an abductee toward the light. And then the dogs' yips and yipes became words.

"Scarlett? Scarlett! I need you to stay with me!"

Lenny? she thought or said. She didn't know which.

"Lenny's here. He's the one who helped me find you. It's going to be okay, Scarlett. I've got you now."

Jesus? She chanced opening her eyes again and when she did, she was greeted by a pair of mismatched eyes—one blue and the other amber mixed with green.

Henry!

She had so many questions to ask, but no strength to ask them. Not yet.

How had he found her? Why had he stopped his race to help her? Didn't he hate her? Hadn't she hurt him beyond redemption?

"Stay with me, Scarlett," he said, wrapping her in a dry blanket and holding her in his arms as he moved around his sled. He raised a cup to her lips and made her drink. The hot liquid lit a fire in her belly, warming her from the inside out. Slowly, she was regaining her strength.

"We need to get you to the hospital, but I don't want to move you until I'm sure you can handle the journey back to the next checkpoint in Safety."

"How?" she asked, finally strong enough to put voice to her words.

"Are you starting to feel better?" he asked with so much hope in his voice. "I'm going to get you some dry boots and socks from my pack."

"How did you find me?" she asked again.

Henry talked to her while he rummaged through the

belongings on his sled. "When I made it to Safety, I made sure to check in on your progress like I'd done for most of the race. I wasn't always on your heels, but I was close enough that I would place as well. When the officials at Safety said you hadn't checked in yet, I knew something was wrong. I waited a bit before I took off back towards White Mountain. There was a break in the weather just long enough for me to hear your team down here."

He returned to her side and worked her boots and socks off, replacing them with the oversized pair in his hands. He finished his story with a smile. "Then I saw Lenny, and he led me to you."

But something about his story didn't make sense. "You turned around and went backward?"

"Yes, I had to. I knew something was wrong. I just felt it. And I knew it would be easier for me to find you on the sled. Easier to retrace your steps."

"But the race, the bucket list, all that money," she argued.

"I told you before and you didn't believe me. Money isn't everything. Some things are so much more important." He dropped a heat pack into each of her boots and then hugged her tight to his chest again.

"But, but, you hate me. I've been so awful to you. Said all those horrible things."

Henry laughed softly and placed a dry kiss on the top of her head. "No, I don't hate you. I have loved you since the first time I ever laid eyes on you, Scarlett. All our bickering, all that hate, it wasn't hate at all. I just want to be near you. I just want to see you happy. If I have to lose the race to protect that, then I will."

"But your family?"

"Will disown me probably, but it won't matter if I have you. Please tell me we can start again. Please give me the chance to show you the real Henry Mitchell, III."

Scarlett said nothing. A part of her was so confused by this declaration and sacrifice by her star-crossed rival, yet another part had always known, had never stopped feeling for him. Could that feeling be love?

"You can't give it all up for me, Henry," she whispered at last. "I'm nobody."

"You're everybody to me. You're the first one who saw me—*me*—not my money or my name. You saw me once, and I'm hoping you can again. The race isn't important. The money isn't important. This, this is what matters." He kissed her head again. "I'll scratch. We both will. We'll go straight to the hospital, and I'll stay by your side until you no longer want me there."

Scarlett had a life-changing decision to make in that moment, and even without thinking it over, she knew exactly what she wanted, what she needed.

"*No*," she said, and Henry's sob rung out into the air.

CHAPTER 43

"I UNDERSTAND." HENRY OPENLY CRIED AS HE SPOKE TO HER now. "At least I'll have tried, and I'd still do it all over again, too. Saving you now is the best thing I've ever done, but I plan to do so much more good with my life now, too. I'll make you proud to have known me."

"No, I don't think you do understand." Scarlett pulled out of his warm arms to look at him face to face. "We're not going to scratch. We're going to finish this race. Together."

"But you need a doctor," he argued, worry setting into his handsome features. Even now, even when he thought she had rejected him, he still wanted to be sure that she would come out of this okay.

"And I have one, at least a future doctor." She smiled at him, hoping he would understand, hoping he would take her words to heart. After all, words had power. "I'm feeling much stronger now. I'll go to the hospital after, but Henry, we are so close. We need to finish this."

"And what… What about us?" He asked the question as if he were afraid to find the answer.

"Well, you were right," she whispered in nervous anticipation of what came next.

His brows furrowed in confusion and his mouth fell open, but no words escaped it.

Scarlett leaned in closer and said, "I *did* want to kiss you that first night, and many times since. Oh, Henry, when I hated you, I loved you." She only took a quick moment to admire the blissful expression that lit up his face. Because she couldn't wait another second when it had already been such a long year. Finally—finally!—she pressed her lips to his in a life-changing, life-giving kiss. At last fire and ice were one, both stronger together.

"I won't let you down. I'll make everything right," Henry promised, happiness dancing in his eyes.

"First, we finish. Then hospital. Then whatever comes next." Scarlett rose to shaky feet, determined and faithful.

"Together?" Henry asked, rising to join her.

"*Together.*"

"Okay. Let's get you to Safety."

The irony that the next checkpoint was named Safety did not escape Scarlett, nor did the sacrifice Henry had made simply for the chance that she would love him in return. She would give him everything, though she had nothing much to offer. He, on the other hand, had forfeited riches, reputation, and possibly the love of his family—all because he considered her the ultimate prize.

After securing her weakest dogs in the two sleds' baskets, Henry helped balance the remaining members of Scarlett's team. And as they continued on, he refused to leave her side, which meant sticking to larger swaths of land as the finished their journey.

At Safety, they dropped some of Scarlett's dogs, leaving her team at just eight now, matching Henry's team which had been winnowed down during the earlier parts of the race. Henry tried a few times to get Scarlett to just finish the race out on his sled, but she remained adamant about needing to finish for herself.

Twenty-two miles later, they reached Nome together, hands clasped between their sleds as at last they crossed the burled arch, completing the race that had changed both their lives and brought them to each other. The race that gave their lives a new light of hope.

It was a race they hadn't won—in fact, they'd finished dead last—but they'd now won so much more. And they'd done it all together.

CHAPTER 44

SCARLETT SAW LAUREN WAITING FOR HER JUST BEYOND THE
Burled Arch. As soon as she'd stepped off from her sled,
Scarlett's friend rushed over to grab her in her arms.

"I was so worried about you. When you didn't come in…
I thought. Oh, Scar. Don't you ever scare me like that again!"
she cried, kissing her friend's cheeks in an almost maternal
way.

Lauren turned on Henry next. "And you!" she shouted
before taking him into her arms, too. "You saved my Scarlett. That makes everything else water under the bridge as
far as I'm concerned."

Scarlett shivered. "D-d-don't say water, please."

"Oh, oh! We need to get you to the hospital. Are you still
in shock? What happened? Tell me everything." She put an
arm around each of them and guided them toward the

nearest building. "You, Henry, tell me everything. Scarlett, just rest up, save your voice."

"I'll be fine, Lauren. The dogs kept me warm until Henry found me. My feet still feel like giant blocks of ice, but I'm fine now."

At the hospital, the doctor informed Scarlett that she was lucky to be alive.

"Don't I know it?" she answered, thanking God once again for how things had turned out. It had taken a disaster to finally bring her and Henry together. Why hadn't she listened to His still small voice before He'd needed to shout?

She did lose a toe to frostbite, but it was a small price to pay for the adventure she'd had. "Big deal. So I won't wear open-toed shoes," she'd told a very concerned Lauren. "My racing days are over anyway."

"What will you do next?" Lauren and Henry said almost in unison.

"Go to the awards banquet to support my friend. It's not too late, is it?"

"Don't you want to enjoy some time out of the spotlight for a change?" Henry asked from his seat beside her in the hospital room.

"Heck no!" she cried. "This is the only Iditarod I'll ever run, and I want to make sure I'm there for the grand finale."

The night of the banquet, she wore the same purple, jeweled dress she'd had on when she'd first met Henry at the previous year's ball. Henry placed a matching silk hankie in his suit pocket to coordinate with her gown and officially declare their newfound couplehood. They arrived together, arm in arm, smiling exhausted smiles but refusing to miss out on the evening by giving an endless series of interviews.

"Henry, is it true you failed the challenge?" a reporter asked.

"I won the only one that matters," he answered, giving Scarlett a quick kiss on the cheek. She could picture the headlines now: *Would-be billionaire trades it all in for love!*

"Do you have any regrets?"

"Just that you're keeping me from this lovely evening. Could we maybe talk later?"

Surprisingly, the press backed off... Only to be replaced by a different mob, and this one was far less happy to see them.

"It's not just your life you're playing with," an elegantly styled woman hissed. "We needed that money, too."

"So you'll buy a smaller mansion on the coast," Henry told his aunt with a shrug.

"How could you?" another family member asked as he shook his head in a more relaxed disappointment.

"Some things are more important than money," Henry answered before dipping Scarlett and giving her a full, dramatic kiss.

When they both came up for air, they saw his family departing with swift, agitated movements.

"Henry, I'm so sorry," she said, not knowing what other words of comfort she could offer in that moment. Just as he'd predicted, his family seemed to have disowned him, leaving him both penniless and nameless in the process.

Henry smiled at her and kissed the top of her head, even though he had to stand on tiptoe to do it. "I don't care. Honestly, it's a relief. Now we can actually enjoy the evening."

And so they made their way through the room full of mushers, many of whom wanted a word with Scarlett, Henry, or both. Previously, Scarlett would've been starstruck or just in awe of all the mushers she'd followed for the past several years. But now, she was in a room of friends and colleagues. She belonged to this crowd, and it welcomed her with open arms.

Lauren, who had finished in fifth place and set a new record for top finishing time by a female musher, had also needed to work hard to make her way through the crowd of congratulatory well-wishers.

At last they made it to their table and sat down together.

"Quite the experience, isn't it?" Henry said to them both as they watched the emcee cross the stage.

"Yeah. I'm just in shock," Scarlett whispered. "I didn't know so many people were rooting for me."

Lauren kept her voice at full volume, however. "People love an under*dog* story. *Heh, heh?* Get it?" She held a hand over her mouth to silence her laughs.

"People love you," Henry said, squeezing Scarlett's hand under the table. "And how could they not?"

They kept their hands clasped in each other's as they watched the winning mushers collect their awards. They clapped and cheered, especially when Lauren accepted her prize, and with it, a hefty purse of prize money.

It all made Scarlett wonder what would be next for her. She'd already decided that this would be her last race, and she'd been fired from her job at the library. So what next? Yes, she got the guy, but they were both broke and unemployed, which meant...

Henry interrupted her then by bringing his face close to her ear and whispering, "I can tell you're thinking really hard about something right now, but look alive. It's almost time for our award."

Scarlett blinked hard at him, but the vision didn't change. "Our award?" she asked.

He kissed her on her forehead and kept his lips there as he growled, "C'mon, bookworm, you can't tell me you don't know about the Red Lantern Award. The prize for finishing last?"

Scarlett still felt foggy and was having a hard time following. "A participation trophy?"

Henry laughed kind-heartedly at her confusion. "Not exactly. I mean, it started off as a gag gift, but mushers soon started to see it as a badge of honor. Overcoming all obstacles and still finishing the race. That sound like anyone you know?"

Sure enough, in the next moment the announcer boomed, "And the winner of the Red Lantern Award this year... We have a tie between Henry Mitchell, III and Scarlett Cole!"

Scarlett blushed as she and Henry took to the stage and claimed the Red Lantern, their own little light for overcoming the big darkness.

Somewhere deep down, she felt the pride Henry had mentioned. There were several mushers that never made it to Nome. Some lost bits of themselves to frostbite like she had, and some had to drop so many dogs they couldn't complete the race. But she had set out to run the Last Great Race and—by golly—she'd finished it.

The evening came to a close, and Scarlett felt nostalgic for this time in her life already, knowing it had now officially ended. It was time for the next great thing, the next adventure. After a few more interviews and lots of goodbyes, she and Henry made their way toward the exit, ready to call it a night.

"Henry, could I have a quick word?" a man Scarlett hadn't seen before said as he approached them both.

"Thaddeus, of course! I'm sure my family has already had several with you." Henry shook the other man's hand. His smile seemed to suggest that this was a welcome interruption. "Scarlett, this is my attorney. Well, my granddad's anyway."

Thaddeus adjusted his cufflinks and chuckled. "Yes, your family did have a lot to say, but they missed something important by leaving early."

Henry raised an eyebrow in disbelief. "Oh, and what's that?"

"Well, according to the stipulations of the will, you didn't need to place in the top ten to complete this bucket list item. You only needed to place."

Henry looked confused as he tried to follow the lawyer's logic, but Scarlett understood it perfectly.

"And he did by winning the Red Lantern!" she shouted.

"Yes, he did," Thaddeus said with a grin. "I always knew you could do it. The estate is yours." He reached out to shake Henry's hand again, and then to shake Scarlett's as well. "You're a wealthy man, Henry Mitchell, III."

"Yes, I am," Henry answered, smiling over at Scarlett. "Yes, I most certainly am."

CHAPTER 45

One year later

THE MONTHS PASSED, AND HENRY AND SCARLETT RETIRED from racing together. At first they'd agreed to give interviews discussing their newfound love and the completion of Henry's Billionaire Bucket List. Soon, though, they began to shrink from the public eye.

Scarlett learned that she'd rather report the news for herself. She started out as a freelancer, but soon had a full-time gig between writing stories about the sport and its players as well as beginning her own adventure novel. She'd read great stories, she'd lived great stories, and now she would write them to share with others.

And even though Henry's family all praised him for

securing their inheritance, he grew more and more distant from them, especially when they so ardantly opposed his decision to donate the largest portion of his wealth rather than keeping it for himself.

"We'll make our own way," he told Scarlett. "We don't need Granddad's tainted money."

He did splurge, though, on an engagement ring for Scarlett. Instead of a diamond, it held an aquamarine and a ruby, each swirling around the other. It reminded her of Henry's eyes, but he said it was fire and ice.

Just like them.

"When I finish medical school, I'm going to marry the heck out of you," he promised when he proposed to her outside of the library with Scarlett's two adopted dogs, Fantine and Cosette, there to share in the moment.

First he gave her the ring, then he handed her a card. "It's yours now," he said before she'd even managed to finish opening the envelope.

Sure enough, he'd donated a hefty some of his money to the library with the stipulation that it would only be used to further education and literacy within the community. He'd also given generously to the Sled Dog Rescue Organization in an effort to undo some of his grandfather's past sins. They could never bring back the dogs that had been tortured and killed, but they could save countless others from facing that same fate—and that meant everything.

Scarlett vowed to tell their stories and joined the board of the SDRO to help make that happen. As promised, she moved into a new apartment with Liz, who was distraught over her father's marriage to the much-hated Vanessa Price.

Henry came for visits once per week. It was the best they could manage while he attended medical school, and she combined both of her greatest passions every day by writing and reading stories about the sport and the dogs she loved so dearly.

And every day, Scarlett made sure to tell Henry how much she loved him because, after all, words had power— and these particular words were the most powerful of all.

Are you ready to read Liz's story next? She just found out that everything she's ever loved is a lie...

CLICK HERE to get your copy of *The Truest Home*, so that you can keep reading this series today!

And make sure you're on Melissa's list so that you hear about all her new releases, special giveaways, and other sweet bonuses.

You can do that here: **MelStorm.com/gift**

WHAT'S NEXT?

Liz Benjamin has lost her place in the world. Not only are her best friends too busy for her, but her father just married a horrible woman who has now moved into their home with her two horrible daughters.

Worse still, a handsome stranger arrives in town for the wedding and starts asking all the wrong questions. With his help, Liz soon finds that everything she thought she knew about herself is based on a terrible lie.

But just how far back does the deception go, and how will finding the truth about Liz's past change her future?

Join Liz, Scarlett, Lauren, and their courageous team of sled dogs in this unforgettable tale of tenacity, trust, and finding where you belong. Start reading THE TRUEST HOME today!

The Truest Home is now available.

CLICK HERE to get your copy so that you can keep reading this series today!

SNEAK PEEK OF THE TRUEST HOME

Liz Benjamin tried to smile as she walked down the petal-strewn aisle toward her father.

He beamed as she moved closer, his expression an unfamiliar mix of nervousness, euphoria, and even pride. This was his special day, and Liz wanted it to be perfect for him...

Even though he was marrying the Wicked Witch of West Anchorage.

As much as Liz despised her soon-to-be stepmother, Vanessa Price, she knew well enough that you couldn't choose who your heart loved. She'd seen that lesson first-hand as her best friend—and now roommate—Scarlett Cole fell head over heels for the heir to the infamous Mitchell estate.

From her seat in the pew, Scarlett gave a thumbs up as Liz passed by on her long walk toward the front of the church. Her new fiancé Henry sat by her side, his fingers laced possessively through hers.

After a couple false starts, Henry had proven himself to be a good man. He had taught both Scarlett and Liz many lessons in their short friendship. For one thing, appearances could be deceiving. And, more importantly than that, a person isn't necessarily destined to follow in his family's footsteps.

Henry certainly hadn't.

And that's what Liz reminded herself often when it came to her new stepsisters, Victoria and Valeria, who would soon follow her down the aisle. Sure, their mother was the very caricature of an evil, money-grubbing politician, but that didn't mean her daughters weren't lovely people in their own right.

When the two families had first met, the two high school girls had kept mostly to themselves, rebuffing any attempt Liz made to hold a conversation. But that could be immaturity—or even shyness—just as much as it could be a cold nature.

Although…

No, Liz had to give them the benefit of the doubt—both for her own sanity and her father's.

As far as she knew, he hadn't gone on a single date since the death of her mother more than twenty-five years ago. Not until he'd met and fallen headlong for Vanessa.

Poor Liz had never gotten the chance to know her mother, who had sadly died in childbirth. It was the one thing she wished she could change about her life. Well, other than the way her father had punished himself by swearing off love for so many years.

He had once told Liz he didn't deserve happiness, but hadn't explained when she pressed him for answers. Her entire life it had been just the two of them, but now three more would be entering their family.

She needed to play nice for her father's sake. Surely he must see something in Vanessa Price that Liz herself hadn't spied yet. She couldn't imagine her dear old dad choosing anyone with less than a pure heart to share his life.

But then again, maybe he had been tricked somehow, pulled into Vanessa's black widow web.

Only, what could she possibly have to gain by going after Ben Benjamin?

None of it made sense to Liz. Maybe one day when she finally fell in love for herself, things would start to make more sense. Maybe Vanessa would change, or maybe she already had without Liz's realizing it.

A wedding was a day to be happy, yet the only emotion that filled Liz's heart that day was fear. She still couldn't decide whether she should be happy her father had finally found a partner or sad by just who that partner ended up being.

When all was said and done, would this truly be the happiest day of her father's life?

Oh, how she hoped so. And that hope was what she would cling to in the absence of any more attractive option.

She looked up and smiled, finally having finished her long walk toward the front of the church and taking her place beside her father. She was his best man, though she wore a dress that matched her sisters' bridesmaids gowns.

Victoria and Valeria floated down the aisle next, arms linked, smiling proudly out at the sea of guests. Their perfect blonde ringlets seemed to shine and reflect the light from the many flashing cameras. Their pale blue, floor-length gowns added to the ethereal image they projected.

Liz looked nowhere near as gorgeous in her dress. The color clashed with her thick auburn hair. The low cut of the neckline showed off the freckles she'd prefer to hide and the cleavage which, quite frankly, didn't really exist.

Her new stepsisters were more than ten years younger than her, yet their bra cups runneth over. God may have granted them beauty and money, but Liz knew she was the one who had truly been blessed, having a father like Ben Benjamin.

She had never wanted for anything growing up, and she didn't want for anything now.

Just for him to be happy with the new path he'd chosen.

As the organist played the first few notes of the "Wedding March," all eyes shifted toward the back of the church where Vanessa Price stood wearing layers and layers of white tulle, a wispy veil that reached straight to the floor, and even a tiara embedded with hundreds of tiny crystals.

Everyone watched the bride as she took smooth, delicate steps toward the altar, but Liz couldn't stop looking at the tears that shone in her father's eyes, the impossibly huge smile that somehow managed to grow even larger.

Happy.

He was finally happy.

And she wouldn't let anyone take that away.

What happens next?
Don't wait to find out...

Read the next two chapters right now in Melissa Storm's free book app.

Or head to my website to purchase your copy so that you can keep reading this sweet, heartwarming series today!

Home Sweet Home

The Sunday Potluck Club

Wednesday Walks and Wags

The Church Dogs of Charleston

A very special litter of Chihuahua puppies born on Christmas day is adopted by the local church and immediately set to work as tiny therapy dogs.

The Long Walk Home

The Broken Road to You

The Winding Path to Love

Alaskan Hearts: Sled Dogs

Get ready to fall in love with a special pack of working and retired sled dogs, each of whom change their new owners' lives for the better.

The Loneliest Cottage

The Brightest Light

The Truest Home

The Darkest Hour

Alaskan Hearts: Memory Ranch

This sprawling ranch located just outside Anchorage helps its patients regain their lives, love, and futures.

The Sweetest Memory

The Strongest Love

The Happiest Place

The First Street Church Romances

Sweet and wholesome small town love stories with the community church at their center make for the perfect feel-good reads!

Love's Prayer

Love's Promise

Love's Prophet

Love's Vow

Love's Trial

Sweet Promise Press

What's our Sweet Promise? It's to deliver the heartwarming, entertaining, clean, and wholesome reads you love with every single book.

Saving Sarah

Flirting with the Fashionista

Stand-Alone Novels and Novellas

Whether climbing ladders in the corporate world or taking care of things at home, every woman has a story to tell.

A Mother's Love

A Colorful Life

Love & War

Do you know that Melissa also writes humorous Cozy Mysteries as Molly Fitz? Click below to check them out:
www.MollyMysteries.com

MEET THE AUTHOR

Melissa Storm is a New York Times and multiple USA Today bestselling author of Women's Fiction and Inspirational Romance.

Despite an intense, lifelong desire to tell stories for a living, Melissa was "too pragmatic" to choose English as a major in college. Instead, she obtained her master's degree in Sociology & Survey Methodology—then went straight back to slinging words a year after graduation anyway.

She loves books so much, in fact, that she married fellow author Falcon Storm. Between the two of them, there are always plenty of imaginative, awe-inspiring stories to share. Melissa and Falcon also run a number of book-related businesses together, including LitRing, Sweet Promise Press, Novel Publicity, and Your Author Engine.

When she's not reading, writing, or child-rearing, Melissa spends time relaxing at her home in the Michigan woods, where she is kept company by a seemingly unending quantity of dogs and two very demanding Maine Coon rescues. She also writes under the names of Molly Fitz and Mila Riggs.

CONNECT WITH MELISSA

You can download my free app here:
melstorm.com/app

Or sign up for my newsletter and receive an exclusive free story, *Angels in Our Lives*, along with new release alerts, themed giveaways, and uplifting messages from Melissa!
melstorm.com/gift

Or maybe you'd like to chat with other animal-loving readers as well as to learn about new books and giveaways as soon as they happen! Come join Melissa's VIP reader group on Facebook.
melstorm.com/group

ACKNOWLEDGMENTS

Where would I bet without my family, my God, or my furry best friends forever?

I certainly wouldn't have been able to bring you this book!

First, I must give thanks to God for putting a story in my heart and giving me the words to tell it.

My greatest earthly support is and will forever be my husband, Falcon, for offering his endless support and unwavering love, even—and especially—when I don't deserve it (like when I have a tight writing deadline and become monster Melissa)! He also helps me with ideas and research and is the one who taught me what true love feels like so that I could write about it and share it with the world.

Oh, I just love that man!

My daughter, Phoenix, is the reason for all that I do. She

is why I write stories of hope and courage and finding one's place. I want her to know that life is a beautiful journey so long as you take it slowly enough to enjoy the view. I hope one day she is able to read my stories and find my love written into every word, line, and page. Because, I promise, it is there.

My beloved pets are also a kind of family and must be thanked. They are the ones who sit next to me day in and day out as I plot my stories and put pen to page. They are the ones I pet and cuddle when the stress of a tight deadline closes in, and they are the first to hear many of my ideas, because there is no shame in talking to your fur babies. They like listening to these stories, too.

My friends and support network are truly one in the same. My indomitable assistant Angi, who is always the most enthusiastic about my work and helps me find the strength and energy to dive deep into my characters' emotions, even when they're hard.

My editor Megan, who builds me up while also deconstructing my prose and somehow inherently knowing what I meant to say even if I accidentally said something else. She's become a true friend, and I'm so excited about what the coming year holds for her!

My designer Mallory is my oldest friend and one I am so happy to have in my life. She is never afraid to tell it like it is, and even though she seems rough and tumble on the outside, she is a tiny, mewmy kitten on the inside.

My proofreader Jasmine helps me so much more than she knows by doing quick and good work, and most importantly, by encouraging Mr. Storm to work on getting his stories into the world.

To all three of the Beckys--the mother, the assistant, and the daughter's imaginary friend who is somehow teaching her Italian. This unlikely trio nurtured my talent growing up, keeps me accountable now that I'm grown, and... teaches my daughter Italian, which is pretty impressive. *Capiche?*

And I always save the best for last. It's you, dear reader. It's you! Thank you for giving my characters and their stories a home in your heart. If a book is written in the forest... but... nobody's around to... read it... Did it ever...?

What I'm trying to say—Megan, help me!—is that I couldn't be who I am without you being who you are. You kind of complete me, and isn't that the greatest love story of all?